"Listen carefully.
I am going to kill you
and take your spirit
straight to Hades if
you don't do as I say."

Flight of the Fire Thief

KINGFISHER

First published 2006 by Kingfisher
This paperback edition first published 2008 by Kingfisher
an imprint of Macmillan Children's Books
a division of Macmillan Publishers Limited
20 New Wharf Road, London N1 9RR
Basingstoke and Oxford
Associated companies throughout the world
www.panmacmillan.com

ISBN: 978-0-7534-1703-4

3 5 7 9 8 6 4 2
2TR/1208/THOM/(SC)/60ABNP/C

A CIP catalogue record for this book is available from the British Library.

Printed in India

Flight
of
the
Fire
Thief

TERRY DEARY

KINGFISHER

ONE

GREECE – ABOUT 4,000 YEARS AGO

I wasn't there myself but I met someone who knows exactly what went on in those days. You will have to trust me when I tell you every word of this story is true... probably. All right, a LOT of it is true. Other bits I may have made up to fill in the gaps so it all makes sense. Yes, you'll see that I tell a lot of lies. But liars are the only people you CAN trust in this world.

Zeus sat on a cloud.

You can do that sort of thing when you're a Greek god. But YOU shouldn't try it. You would need a very long ladder to get up to the clouds and as soon as you stepped off you would probably fall clean through the cloud. This can be very messy – especially if someone is walking underneath you.

Only special people like me and my pa could sail up and over the clouds. How could I do that? Wait and see.

Where was I? Oh, yes, Zeus on his cloud. He wore wings and was the most beautiful thing you've ever seen – so beautiful ordinary people (like you and me) couldn't bear to look at him.[1]

Next to Zeus sat his wife Hera and she was not so beautiful because she had a scowl on her face. Her nose crinkled like a caterpillar's back and her lips were as thin as an ant's leg.

"You promised me a holiday," she snapped.

"This is a holiday, dearest," Zeus smiled. "A sparkling blue sea and miles of sandy beach."

"The beach is covered with human corpses!" she screeched.

"There's a war on, my lovely," her husband shrugged. "We can sit and watch it just as those humans watch their little plays in the theatre."

Hera pouted. "I wouldn't know. You never take me to the theatre."

1 "Aha!" you cry. "Last week I was starving and a cheese sandwich was the most beautiful thing I've ever seen! More beautiful than a Greek god." All I can say is this: if you keep crying out like that I'll never get on with my story. So stop arguing and listen.

"This is real life – much more fun," he argued. "We can even join in."

"You are too mean to take me to the theatre. You're so mean you'd steal a dead fly from a blind spider."

"Only if you were feeling hungry," he muttered.

Hera didn't hear. Just as well.

"The town stinks," she said. "Humans stink. I don't know why you don't just send down a thunderbolt and burn it to the ground. A good fire would clean it up."

"Ah, fire," Zeus nodded. "They don't need my fire. The humans can make fire for themselves."

Hera turned to him with a face as sharp as a shrew. "And who *gave* them the power of fire?"

"I know," Zeus sighed.

Hera slapped and plumped up the cloud to make herself more comfortable. "I asked you a question, Zeus. Who gave them fire?"

"My cousin Prometheus," Zeus said and closed his eyes. He was wishing he hadn't mentioned it.

"Yes, your cousin Theus! He stole fire from the gods and gave it to those creeping little, fighting little, *stinking* little humans."

"Don't get on at me. I have punished him…" Zeus began.

"Oh, you *punished* him. You had him chained to a rock. And every day the Avenger came down in the shape of an eagle and ripped out his liver. What sort of punishment is that?" Hera snapped and thundery sparks crackled in the cloud.

"Every night the liver grew back so he had to suffer the agony every day for two hundred years…" Zeus argued and grew angry as the cloud grew dark.

"But what happened? Eh? What happened?" Hera sneered. "You let him escape!"

"I didn't exactly *let* him…"

"All right. You let Heracles *rescue* him. Same difference. And where is Theus now? Hiding. He's travelled through time and space and he could be anywhere. The poor little Avenger has worn out its wings seeking for him!"

"*Poor*? *Little*? It's a blooming great bird with the sharpest beak this side of Mount Olympus. Its talons can rip a rhino's skin…"

"Don't argue with me, Zeus. You always lose," Hera said with a shake of her head. "Theus gave fire to the humans and he got away with it. I only hope the Avenger finds him one day. It's still out there searching!"

Zeus propped himself up on an elbow. "I *did* make Theus a promise, my dear. I gave him a challenge. I said that if he could find one true human hero I'd forgive him!"

Hera snorted… then her nose twitched as the stink from the city slipped into her nostrils. "He'll fail. He'll never find a human hero. The Avenger will find Theus first."

"The Avenger will be a bit busy, my dear," Zeus said and peered over the edge of the cloud to the city by the sea below. "There will be a lot of warriors here who need to be taken down to Hades and the Underworld. I'm tired of this Troy."

"You're like a baby," Hera laughed bitterly. "You soon get tired of a toy."

"I said *Troy*, not *toy*," Zeus sniffed. "The Greeks have been trying to take the city for *ten years* now – *that's* not getting tired *quickly*! Ten *years*!"

Hera rolled over and lay on her stomach next to her husband. The gods gazed down.

Inside the city the ragged Trojans trudged the streets, thin and weary from the endless war. With secret tunnels, and hidden doors, enough food had slipped into the city to keep them going for ten years.

Bottomless wells of sweet water would last them forever. But the spirit of the people was as threadbare as their clothes. They longed for freedom. Freedom from a city that had become a prison – freedom from the fear that their prison walls would fall and let in sharp, slicing, stabbing death.

There were no rats in the city of Troy. They'd all been eaten long ago.

Outside the city a thousand Greek ships rested and rotted on the hot shore. Tattered tents stood, faded and patched, flapping in the warm wind that blew over the soft sands. Slouching soldiers sat on rocks, polished their worn weapons for the three-thousand and six-hundredth time and longed for home.

"So, what are you going to do about it, husband?" Hera asked.

"Put an end to it," Zeus said.

Hera nodded. "And would you like me to tell you who is going to win?"

Zeus's shoulders dropped. "You are going to anyway."

Hera gave a small smile like a cat that's cornered a bowl of milk. "The Greeks are going to enter Troy. They are going to kill the pathetic Prince Paris and his hideous Helen."

"I thought you might say that," Zeus muttered. Hera held a big grudge against Paris and Helen. Ten years ago the goddesses held a beauty contest and Prince Paris was the judge. Hera offered the judge power over all of Asia. Athena, goddess of war, offered him victory wherever he fought. Aphrodite, goddess of love, offered him the gift of the most beautiful woman in the world. And everyone knew that was Helen of Sparta.

Paris chose Aphrodite as the winner and won the hand of Helen. Hera chose to sulk.

"I hate Helen! Hate her, *hate her*, *HATE HER!*" she cried.

"You don't like her then?" Zeus smiled.

"I can't TELL you how much I hate her," she screamed and the cloud shivered and shook out a storm of raindrops onto the dusty heads of the Trojans underneath. "She is *not* the most beautiful woman in the world – her hair is too straight, her nose is too short and as for her ears… well, what can I say about a woman with ears like that?"

"And she's married to Menelaus, of course," Zeus added, stoking up his wife's rage.

"Ooooh! Yes! A faithless woman. Married to poor King Menelaus and still she ran off with Paris of Troy." Hera pulled back her lips in a savage sneer. "Her Troy boy!" she said and looked pleased with her little joke. "And just look at the trouble she's caused," she added with a sweep of her hand at the scene below. "A thousand ships and fifty thousand soldiers sent to take her back to Greece. Me? I'd leave her to rot in Troy. From the smell of the place it is rotting already."

Zeus sniffed and nodded.

Hera turned quickly to Zeus. "So? Whose side are you going to join? If you let *Troy* win then I will make you wish you lived in Hades with all the tortures the humans suffer there after death."

Zeus held up his mighty hands. "Oh, don't worry, wife. Troy will *lose* because the old curse says Paris will bring about the destruction of the city. We can't go against the old curses," Zeus said.

"The old curse also says the Greek hero Achilles will die at Troy." She jabbed a finger at the Greek tents on the plains of Troy. "He's still alive."[2]

2   Hera and Zeus could SEE Achilles wandering round the camp because they had incredible eyesight. If you could fly, like me, you would see people on the ground like ants. But the gods had eyes like telescopes (binoculars?). Amazing but true.

Zeus rubbed his eyes tiredly. "Yes, there's so much to do. I don't know where to start."

"Send for the Avenger," Hera told him. "It'll be handy to have it around when Achilles and Paris are killed. The Avenger can take them straight to Hades."

Zeus nodded, placed his fingers to his lips and gave a whistle that shook the walls of Troy. It also made Hera's ears ring.

"Must you?"

"I have to send for Hermes, our messenger."

"Right. *Then* you need to arrange for Achilles to die… and *then* you have to make sure the Greeks get into Troy and kill Paris."

Zeus nodded slowly. "Yes, that's what I need to do," he agreed.

Hera puffed out her cheeks and blew with pride – that caused a sandstorm on the beach and tattered the tents again. "Phoo! I honestly don't know *what* you'd do without me, Zeus," she said.

"I'd like a chance to find out," he muttered under his breath.

"What was that?"

"I said, dear, I think you've blown some fires out!"

"Fires out? What are you on about Zeus?"

"Nothing, dear," the great god said then turned as he heard a fluttering of wings. A young man landed on the cloud, wearing a satchel at his waist. He held a wooden rod with snakes twined around it. There were wings on his sandals and wings on his helmet and a spoilt look on his face. "Ah, here's Hermes," Zeus said.

"What do you want this time, my foul father?" Hermes sighed.

Zeus took a deep breath and kept his temper. It wasn't easy.

"I want you to find the Avenger and bring it to Troy."

Hermes threw down his rod and the shocked snakes hissed their surprise. "Ooh! He wants me to find the Avenger. Just like that? I say, just like that?"

Zeus punched the cloud in anger... but punching clouds doesn't do you much good. He began to speak quickly in a low, angry voice. "Hermes, you are the messenger of the gods and it is your job to take messages. So will you please stop complaining about it and get on with what you are paid to do?"

Hermes blinked. "Paid? When have you ever *paid* me. I am rushed off my winged feet, morning to night and night to morning. And not *only* do I not get paid but I don't even get any *thanks*. All I get is shouted at!" He pulled at the hem of his tunic and blew his nose on it.

"You've made Hermes cry now," Hera groaned. "Say you're sorry, Zeus."

"You're sorry, Zeus," the god growled then turned back to the snivelling messenger. "Hermes. *Please* do this small thing for me and I will be so very grateful I will never shout at you again."

"Promise?" Hermes sniffed.

"Promise," Zeus said. "The Avenger is travelling through time looking for cousin Theus. Theus and the Avenger were last seen in a place called Eden city in a time they call 1858."

"Time? I have to travel through time!" Hermes screeched.

"We'll be *so-o* very grateful," Hera told him. "We'll have a special party for you when you get back."

Hermes's face lit up. "A party? With fairy cakes?"

"Yes, dear," Hera said. She picked up the hissing rod and handed it to him. "Now, off you go, through time. Tell the Avenger we're at Troy."

As Hermes's wings began to beat like a humming bee Zeus waved, "Have a nice *time*!"

Hera rubbed her hands. "That's that problem solved. Now… *how* are you going to kill Achilles?" she asked.

Zeus smirked. "I have a rather neat little plan, my dear. A brilliant plan, a work of a genius, even if I do say so myself."

"Hmm!" Hera said. "We'll see."

Somewhere, just beyond the farthest star, the Greek demi-god Prometheus drifted on white wings.

It was lonely out there. He headed for home.

Two

East River City – 1795

This time I really WAS there. This is my story so I know it happened. I was just a 12-year-old girl at the time but I remember it as clearly as if it was the day before yesterday... even though it was over sixty years ago. I may be getting old, but there are some things you NEVER forget. And being shot by my own pa is one of them...

I used to hate it when Pa shot me. Sometimes he did it twice a day and that made me hurt all over.

That windy afternoon in East River City was no different. I'd been up since daybreak helping to fill the balloon with hot air. By afternoon it was higher than a ten-storey building and straining at the ropes that held it to the earth in the city park.

Pa had painted the white paper balloon with red stripes and great black letters told the world, "Dr Dee and his amazing Carnival of Danger!"

The people of East River City couldn't miss it and they were starting to gather in the park. Kids with runny noses formed queues to buy my apples dipped in candy or my sugar canes, my pop-corn and my sugar almonds. "We should charge people to see the show," I grumbled one day.[3]

"No need, Nellie," he laughed. "If people have to pay to come they'll stay away. Tell them they're getting something for *nothing* and they'll flock along. That makes it easier to take their money when they get here! People are suckers like that," he said and tapped the side of his nose. He did that to show he was the wisest man in the world. He wasn't.

So we made our money by selling cheap food at five times what it was worth and passing a hat around the crowd after each amazing danger. The people paid

---

3 I did a lot of grumbling. This is NOT because I am a moaner. It's because Pa gave me a lot to grumble about. If your pa shot you twice a day then YOU would grumble and whine a lot more than I do. You look like a grumbler and a whiner to me so don't you go complaining if I moan from time to time!

up. I remember that afternoon and the kid in the sailor suit. "Hey!" he squawked. "I bit into this apple and found a worm!"

"Wow!" I gasped. "You lucky, lucky boy! That's a rare apple you have there."

"It is?"

"Why, yes. Only one apple in a hundred has a magic worm inside it. We usually charge *double* for apples with a magic worm inside."

"Magic? What does it do?" the kid asked.

"Do? Why... it... it... has the power to make you invisible," I told him.

He looked down at his sailor suit. "I can still see me," he argued.

"Ah, you have to wait till midnight then ask the worm nicely." I knew that by midnight we'd be miles away and he'd never get his money back. Pa's rule was, never give the suckers their money back.

The kid looked at the apple. "But I bit it in half," he frowned.

"Ah! Shame! Then you'll never get to be invisible," I sighed. "You really should have been more careful," I scolded. "Now, are you going to pay me double for that special apple or do I have to tell your ma and pa you tried to sneak off with a magic apple without paying?"

The kid turned pale. "N-no!"

I held out my hand. His trembling little paw pressed a coin into mine. He backed away, scared as a rabbit in a dog's dinner bowl.

Feel sorry for the kid, do you? Pa told me never to feel sorry for the suckers. But I guess I have a soft inside to my tough outside. I would *never* tell Pa this, but that afternoon I felt a touch of real pity for the poor little worm that got eaten in half.

It's a tough life.

"Time to close the stall and get ready for the show, Nellie," Pa said.

"Don't call me Nellie," I muttered.

"It's your name," he lied.

You see, my name is Helen. Some clever person decided it would be funny to turn the name backwards and girls called 'Helen' often get called 'Neleh'... or Nellie. Now I didn't mind Helen and I could live with 'Nell' but I never liked 'Nellie'. So, if it's all right with you, I'll call myself Nell in this story so you don't get confused with the other Helen... the one with a face so beautiful they launched a thousand ships to find her.[4]

"Call me Nell, Pa," I said. "Or I won't do the show."

He knew I meant it. Me and Pa got on well because we'd learned how to handle one another. Pa may tell the world he had the most amazing Carnival of Danger but we both knew that I was the one who did the dangerous bits. He was just the showman that sold them.

I swept up the cloth with the candy and dropped it into the basket of the balloon. I checked that the fire below the balloon was smoking nicely and ducked down to change into my first costume. It was a baggy silk suit striped blue and yellow, a black moustache and black boots.

I needed those boots to save my soles. Being shot by your pa can hurt your heels and slap your sole till you're sore.

By the time I was ready, Pa was standing on a box and calling to the crowd.

"Welcome to Doctor Dee's most amazing Carnival of Danger!" he roared. He had a good voice did Pa.

4   Yes, dear reader, even though we were born 4,000 years apart, me and Helen of Troy would end up in the same tale. Of course I was more beautiful than Helen of Troy – I mean, when you get to 4,000 years old you must have a few wrinkles.

"This afternoon you will see my talented team of plucky performers daring to defy death."

He had the crowd gripped now. They'd fallen silent and he was able to lower his voice. "In fact, my friends, I have to warn you some of them may *not* survive the dangers. Some days Death wins. If you are upset by the sight of mangled bodies and bleeding corpses then please go home now…"

Of course no one moved. The suckers went to our shows *hoping* to see some disasters. Our aim was to disappoint them. At least that was *my* aim. You see there was no talented 'team' of plucky performers. There was just me. Little Nellie Dee. I did all the stunts. Dr Dee's Amazing Carnival of Danger was me and Pa. I just changed costumes and wigs under the cover of the balloon basket while Pa kept the crowd's attention with the big build-ups.

"And, for our first, death-defying display we have… all the way from Russia…" (pause while the crowd goes, 'Ooh!') "… the magnificent… the masterful… the miraculous… Gregory… the-e-e-e… Grrrreat!"

I stepped forwards and bowed stiffly to the cheering crowds but kept moving quickly so they couldn't see the ribbons that held my moustache in place or the high heels on the boots that made me look taller.

I stood next to the wooden cannon and faced the dark muzzle. I gripped it, raised myself up, placed my feet inside the barrel and let myself slide down. As I slid into the gloom I twisted so I was face down. (I hated it when I shot out on my back and found myself looking up at the clouds.)

Pa's voice and the cheering of the crowd was muffled down there. I knew he was going on about the danger of me breaking my neck if he fired the cannon and I missed the safety net. Pa was a great liar but that bit was true!

He always made out it was a real cannon filled with gunpowder. In fact it was a wooden cannon with a big spring. When he lit the fuse he burned through a piece of cord that held the spring back. When the cord burned through, the spring sprang and threw me out. There was a flash and a pop and I was flying.

Now Pa's a phoney and a faker but he's good at his job. He always made sure I hit that net. As I grew older and heavier he changed the power of the spring and never made any mistakes. I was too precious. After all, where would he find another cannon-ball if he

killed me? Especially after what happened to Ma…
but that's another story.

Yet that afternoon in East River City was cursed. It
could have been the east wind that whipped over the
sea or it could have been our luck had to run out
some time.

Inside the barrel of the wooden cannon I heard the
sizzle of the fuse and screwed up my face, waiting for
the shock of the spring smacking into my feet.

Sizzle… twing^5… whoosh… thunk!

I felt the sting on my feet. The barrel was smooth
and waxed. My costume was silk, so rushing out didn't
graze me or burn me. Then the air filled my lungs
with a great rush as if someone was stuffing a pillow
down my throat. My moustache slapped my cheeks
and my eyes watered.

Then I reached the top of my curve and slowed.
This was where I'd tuck up my knees, do a somersault
to make the crowd gasp then spread my arms and legs,
like a flying frog, to drop into the net… usually.

But that afternoon the wind was from my right

5   This is the sound of the cord snapping – it's a cross between a singing
and a twanging. A twing, in fact. You may not have heard this word before.
You have now.

side. Pa *never* allowed that to happen. The wicked wind must have switched direction. I felt myself being pushed to the left of the net. I twisted in the air and rolled to my right like a spinning bullet.

Even at that height I heard the crowd gasp. *This* was what they'd come to see… a Russian cannon-ball a-rushin' to the ground. I thought I was a goner. Was this how the worm felt as the kid's teeth crunched into the apple?

I twisted again and used my legs to kick out and swim against the air. The edge of the net was almost out of reach as I hurtled towards it. I snatched at it and got my right hand on the edge and held tight.

The force almost tore my arm out of my shoulder and I had to let go. I dropped to the ground but had slowed myself enough to save my life. That's not to say it didn't hurt. It did. I landed on my feet and the blow almost rattled my teeth out of my head. My wig and moustache were twisted and all I could think was to set them straight, take a bow and rush back to the balloon to change.

My knees were weak – either from the shock or the fall – and I wobbled away to the balloon basket as the crowd cheered.

I flung off the blue and yellow costume and dressed in a pink ballet dress to appear as Miss Cobweb from England. I climbed up onto the high wire and danced along the tightrope. The wind pushed me and when I leaned towards it the wind dropped and left me tottering. I always liked to put in the odd totter to excite the crowd, but that day it was for real.

As Captain Dare, in a tight black swimming suit and leather helmet, I dived from a high platform into a shallow pool of water. Just for fun the water was covered in a film of burning oil that roared in the wind. A gust blew me hard towards the left, so I jumped to the right and hoped it would blow me back towards the small circle of flaming water. As I threw myself off the board, the wind dropped a little and let me fall dangerously close to the right side. Somehow I hit the pool and pulled myself out. This time I dressed myself in dungarees, cotton shirt and canvas jacket. Pa climbed in beside me. "You did well, Nell," he muttered. He jangled a leather bag full of cash and stored it carefully in the bottom of the basket. "We can't take the balloon up in this wind," I hissed.

"We can. Trust me, I'm a doctor," he shrugged.

"A what?"

"A doctor! Doctor Dee!" he explained.

"No you're not! You just invented that name! You're not *really* a doctor of science or anything else!" I reminded him.

"Maybe not," he shrugged. "We'll be all right… we'll just take her up a little way," he promised. Then he began announcing our final 'Danger'.

"My friends… you will now witness the first ever flight by a human being in this country. Direct from Paris this balloon was built by the Montgolfier Brothers themselves…"

The wind was whining in the ropes that held it to the basket. The ropes were tight as the balloon strained to lift upwards. The wind was making the straw-and-wool fire burn too hot.

"We can't take the balloon up!" I groaned at Pa. He wasn't listening. He had already chosen four heavy men in the audience to pull us back down after we'd risen a hundred feet in the air.

"Prepare to watch and wonder!" he cried and pulled the slip knot that set us free.

The balloon rose like a rocket and threw us down into the basket. We soon reached the end of the rope that tied us to the ground. The speed was too great.

The rope snapped. The four men found they were being lifted off the ground so they dropped their ropes and set us free. One tried to tie his rope to our cannon but, being made of wood, it had no weight.

The crowd on the ground below was just a blur of gaping faces. We were in free flight for the first time ever.

"Oh dear," Pa sighed. "Oh dear, oh dear, oh *dear*!"

I looked over the side and saw the city slip away below us. "Great," I groaned. "Doctor D... D for disaster."

THREE

TROY — ABOUT 4,000 YEARS AGO

There are two stories going on here. At some time — I don't know when — they will join up to make one story. Now I don't want you to forget what was going on back in Greece. So we'll leave me floating off to disaster in the balloon... don't worry about me, I'll survive somehow... and we'll go back to the plot to smash Troy.

Paris stood on the walls of his palace and pouted. "I wish those Greeks would go away," he sighed.

"You say that every day," Helen reminded him. Her face had been lovely enough to launch a thousand ships. But ten years of frowning had creased that face a bit. These days she'd have been be lucky to launch nine hundred ships.

"It's that Achilles," Paris said. "He's such a hero he'll *never* give up."

"You say *that* every day too," Helen said. "You could be getting a teeny bit boring, Paris dear. I ran away from Menelaus because *he* was so boring."

"And because he never washed his feet, you said. He was a smelly old man," Paris reminded her.

"And when did you last wash *your* feet, Paris my petal?"

He sniffed. "Last week… I'm saving on soap. There's a war on, you know."

"I know… oh, I know," Helen muttered. "I'm just off to see my dress-maker," she said and glided along the platform behind the wall like an elegant lady. A lady so elegant she could launch at least eight hundred ships with that windburned face.

"If only I could get rid of Achilles," Paris muttered.

"You *could*," a Trojan soldier said.

If Paris had been paying attention then he'd have noticed there was no Trojan soldier there a moment ago. A sprinkle of cloud-dust had fallen behind him and taken the shape of a warrior.

Now *you* know that soldier was really Zeus who had shape-shifted – but Paris wasn't very bright and he was too worried and wearied by war to notice.

"Could what, captain?" Paris asked.

"Oh, mighty Paris, sir, my lord, I be only a poor and 'umble sergeant, I be not one of your great and good cap'ns, your holiness!" Zeus said.[6]

"Did you know, sergeant, Helen told me that my feet smell? What do you think of that?"

"With all respect, mighty Paris, I be thinking 'er ladyship she be mistaking herself. Why, every Trojan tramp and tickle-monger[7] would tell you that feet don't smell. Lordy, no sir. It be noses what smells, sir! Not feet! Feet's for walking on, not for smelling. Why if your ole feet smelled then every time you stepped in a pile of horse droppings in the street you'd…"

"Thank you, sergeant. Can you tell me how to get rid of Achilles?"

"I'm glad you asked me that, sir. As it be happening,

6   Yes, I know this is a curious and ungodly way to talk. But there were two reasons for it. Firstly Zeus was only guessing how a Trojan sergeant might talk. Secondly Zeus enjoyed a bit of play-acting, so he always went a bit over the top when he appeared to humans. Let's be honest – he was just a god-awful actor.

7   A Trojan tickle-monger was a clown who sold tickles to his audience… in Troy. Sadly they died out in Roman times when tickling was made illegal by the emperor Vespasian and tickle-mongers were thrown to the crocodiles in the Coliseum.

I be knowing a way to be doing away with the awful Achilles," Zeus said.

"By Zeus, you're a better man than me if you can do it!" Paris said and slapped the god on his back.

"There be a legend about that there Achilles, there be, sir…"

"I know it!" Paris sighed. "His mother was Thetis…"

"Nice lass," Zeus nodded.

"You knew her?"

"Well!"

"Anyway, Thetis was a goddess and she wanted her son Achilles to be safe in battle. So, when he was a baby, she dipped him in the river Styx in the Underworld. That way he couldn't be harmed. But…"

"Ah, *but…*" Zeus went on, "she held him by the heel…"

"And the heel was the only part that wasn't touched by the charmed waters," Paris finished.

"So?" Zeus nodded.

"So what?"

Zeus rolled his eyes. This Paris wasn't very bright. "*So-o-o…* if someone was going to attack him then *where* would they attack him?"

Paris scratched his head under his long and flowing hair. "Er? In bed when he's asleep?"

"No… I mean, where on his body would you strike him? You'd have to strike him on the heel – his weak spot."

Paris blinked. "*ME* strike him? Who says *I'm* going to strike him?"

Zeus sighed. "No one else is going to do it for you, my great and mighty lord."

"He's a wondrous warrior. I might get hurt!" Paris argued. "Did you not see what he did to our greatest fighter Hector? First he killed him, had his corpse dragged round Troy, then he fed him to the dogs! I don't want to end up as doggy-dinner, thank you very much!"

"You won't. Not if you use a sneaky plot, sir."

"Ah, I'll have to think of one."

"I have one, mighty lord."

"You have? Good man… er, what is it?"

And Zeus told him.

That was why, two days later…

… Achilles arrived at the palace of Princess Polyxena.

All marble and flaming torches.[8] Very smart but smoky and cold on your bare feet.

A trumpet sounded as Achilles entered the great hall. Princess Polyxena sat on a couch and jammed her pretty fingers in her pretty ears. That trumpet could be a real pain.

There were just two other people in the room that Achilles could see... one was dressed as a Trojan sergeant – the enemy! He stood in a shadowy corner but Achilles knew no common soldier would dare to attack him.

Next to the sergeant stood a strange, hunched figure in a cloak that could almost have been a very tall eagle. Achilles was sure he could see a sharp, curved beak poking out from under its hood. Something about that figure made even Achilles shiver a little.

The trumpet stopped. "Thank god for that!" Polyxena sighed. "Now you must be the famous Achilles, are you?" she asked.

Achilles looked surprised. "No one else has this armour, made by the gods," he cried and looked as

8   The palace was all marble and flaming torches, not Achilles. I want you to picture the scene so I have to put in bits like that. It's what writers do.

mighty as he could – you *know*, left hand on his heart, right hand stretched out with a heavy sword waving around. "No one but Achilles has this armour that glows with the power of Mount Olympus."

"Oh, I don't know anything about armour," Princess Polyxena giggled. "I'm more into frocks myself. Have you ever tried wearing a frock?"

A strange thing happened to Achilles. He seemed to shrink a little – like a hot air balloon with a puncture. His face turned red and he couldn't look the pretty princess in the face. "Maybe," he mumbled.

Polyxena smiled a wicked smile. "I did hear something about you dressing up as a girl and pretending to be your sister. Is that right?"

"Yes," Achilles whispered.

"Your mum dressed you as a girl so you could escape from a battle without getting killed, didn't she?"

"Yes."

"Your mum really looks after you, doesn't she, Achilles? Saving your life in a battle by dressing you as a girl. Dipping you in the river Styx to stop you getting hurt. Quite a mummy's boy, aren't you, Achilles?"

Silence.

"*Aren't* you, Achilles?"

"Yes."

"I couldn't hear you… the trumpets make me a little deaf. Say it again – louder."

"*Yes!*"

"Louder!"

"*YES!*"

Polyxena smirked. "Now you've come here to ask for my hand in marriage," she said.

"A messenger said you fancied me," Achilles said.

"And *do* you fancy me?"

"You're very pretty," the warrior nodded.

"As pretty as Helen of Troy? A woman whose face can launch a thousand ships?"

"Prettier – they say her tired face could hardly struggle to launch seven hundred ships these days!" Achilles chuckled.

"Turn around," Polyxena ordered.

"What?"

"What? Has the trumpet made you deaf too? I said turn around. I want to see what you look like from the back," she said.

"The back?" he asked.

"Yes, you know – the side that isn't the front," she said impatiently. "Turn around."

Achilles turned. The princess leaned down and looked under her couch. "Right, Paris, fire the poisoned arrow!" she hissed quietly.

"Ooh!" came a groan from the gloom. "It's not easy, lying under here and trying to use my bow! And my hands are all numb and cold with lying on this marble floor."

"Get on with it!" Polyxena ordered.

There was a twang and an arrow slithered out from under the couch. It skittered over the hard floor and hit the trumpeter on the toe. He gave a small gasp and fell to the floor with a clatter of brass trumpet.

Achilles looked over his shoulder. "What was that?" he asked.

Polyxena waved a hand. "Nothing, Achilles. You've just had an arrow escape. Turn around and *don't* look back unless I tell you." She ducked her head under the couch and said, "It'll have to be the poison dagger, Paris. Get him."

"Ooh! I'm so stiff. I bet I catch my death of cold after this."

"Get *ON* with it!" Polyxena moaned.

Paris crawled out and wriggled over the floor like a snake.

Zeus and the cloaked figure beside him went as still as the marble pillars in the hall. Still as the trumpeter. Still as his clattered and battered trumpet.

Paris reached the feet of Achilles, took a deep breath and lashed out with the poison dagger.

Achilles raised his foot off the ground, half turned and saw Paris looking up, fear in his eyes. Achilles raised his sword to strike. He swayed. He sighed softly. He fell over backwards.

His famous armour clanged like bells and his sword crashed like a cymbal. "God!" Polyxena cried. "That's worse than the bleeding trumpet noise!"

Zeus turned to the hooded figure next to him. "There you are, Avenger. One gone, one more to go."

"One more?" the creature hissed through its beak.

"Paris. We still need to make sure *Paris* dies. Then this whole Trojan war can end and we can all go home," Zeus explained.

"I have to hang around till Paris dies?"

"You may as well. Make sure they both go down to Hades in the Underworld together – it's always nice to have a bit of company in the Underworld."

The Avenger tapped its foot and its sharp, eagle claws clattered on the marble floor. "What about your cousin Prometheus? You made it my duty to find Prometheus. To bring him back and chain him to the Caucasus mountain." The Avenger was breathing quicker now. "To visit him every day and tear out his liver!"

"You have to find him first," Zeus reminded him.

"He was in a place called Eden City," the Avenger squawked. "Four thousand years in the future. I was so close to catching him. I *know* he'll return there. I *know* it. I have to go forwards in time and find him."

Zeus sighed. "There's time enough for that later. For now let's get Paris killed and get him and Achilles down to Hades."

"Then I will fly to Eden City," the Avenger spat.

Prometheus on his white wings saw a green and blue planet ahead of him. A small silver moon hung above it. "Home," he sighed. "Maybe Zeus will forgive me."

FOUR

FLYING OVER EDEN CITY – 1795

You'll remember I was left in a runaway balloon, flying over East River City… you DO remember that, don't you? Pay attention if you don't. Over in Paris some people had flown free like that – people like the Roberts Brothers – but usually they just put a sheep, a duck and a cockerel in the basket. We were the first humans to fly in our country.

Pa stood at the edge of the basket and looked down. I know he was a showman and a bit of a crook but I had to admire him then. He wore his top hat pulled down firmly on his thick grey hair so it didn't blow

---

9   It's true. Look it up in some dusty old history book. I can understand why they would send up a flying sheep. But why a duck? Ducks can fly for themselves. Those balloon pioneers were odd people. But on with the story…

40

away. The long tails of his black coat and the red-and-white striped cravat whipped around in the wind… red, white and black were the colours of the balloon, of course, and we always thought of them as "our" colours. Now we were going to die in our colours.

Yet Pa stayed quite calm in the rocking basket.

"We're going to die!" I cried.

He turned and smiled at me. "Yes, Nell, we are going to die some day."

"I mean *this* day! We're going to die very soon when we crash!" I shouted.

Pa thought about this carefully. "Maybe. Maybe not. We're still alive now, aren't we?"

"Yes, but…"

"Then hang on to hope, Nell, hang on to hope!"

My cheeks were cold and I realized there were tears running down them. I wiped them away angrily. If Pa wasn't going to panic then I wasn't.

I looked over the side of the basket down to East River City below. It was a very *neat* city. The fields were square patches of green and yellow, grass and corn. The parks had ponds and shady, tree-lined paths. The streets were straight and the sea to the east was calm and sparkling.

The expressions on the upturned faces of the crowd were too small to see now and wisps of cloud blew through the ropes that held the basket.

Pa threw some straw and sheep's wool into the metal fire-box over our heads. "That'll make us go even higher!" I said. "We'll end up on the moon!"

"Better than ending up in the river," he laughed.

"What river?"

I moved quickly across to his side of the basket and it rocked and almost tipped. Far below was a greasy, grey river, sluggish as a slug and twice as cold. The east wind was carrying us over it now.

"This is the river Eden," he explained. "On the east bank is East River City," he explained.

"So we're heading for the west bank? What's there?" The cloud round the balloon was blotting out the way ahead.

"Eden City," Pa said.

"Eden City?" I'd heard the name. We'd been to most of the big cities to give our shows but never to Eden City. "Why have we never been there before?" I asked.

"No one goes to Eden City," Pa explained. He sat down in the basket so he was out of the clammy damp of the cloud. He unwrapped a small packet of bread and cheese and we shared it. With my cloth full of candy apples and sugar canes we wouldn't starve. I smiled to think those apple-worms were probably the first worms in the world to fly into the clouds!

"Eden City is as far to the west as our people have gone. They built the city and tried to set off into the plains beyond. But they were stopped by the Wild People."

"Who are they, Pa?"

"The people who were here before we landed from Europe."

"They wouldn't be very pleased to see us, I guess?"

"No," he said and laughed. "They were wild! First they drove back the pioneers who tried to make their farms on the plains. Then they headed for Eden City. They have lots of tribes and thousands of warriors. They all came together to surround Eden City."

"Then they must have captured it," I said. "If we land there we'll be prisoners of the Wild People!"

Pa shook his head. "Eden City built great wooden walls to keep the Wild warriors out. The Wild People are surrounding Eden City – not many people can get in or out. An odd ship gets through with food.

Just enough to keep them going. It's a siege and it's been going on ten months now."

"They must be great fighters to keep out the Wild People," I said.

Pa pulled a face to show he doubted it. "We have metal. We have guns and we have bullets – the Wild People just have stone axes. Wooden bows and stone-tipped arrows. Eden City can't kill ten thousand Wild warriors – but the Wild warriors can't fight musket-fire. It's what they call a stalemate. The siege could go on a long, long time."

"And that's where we're headed?"

"If we make it over the wide river," Pa said. I noticed the air was clearer and we were dropping down out of the clouds now.

That's when I saw Eden City for the first time. East River City was a patchwork quilt of green and gold, autumn brown set in a brilliant blue sea.

Eden City was a pile of grey-brown sludge. Tall buildings rose like rotten teeth from blackened gums. Even in the autumn gale a fog of grimy smoke hung over the place like a dirty blanket over a corpse.

"There's nowhere to land!" I told Pa as we slipped down into the gloom. "The streets are too narrow.

The buildings are too high. We'll smash into them and die!"

"Stop talking about dying, Nell. Trust me, I'm a doctor," he said and reached for a handle over his head.

This time I didn't give him an argument about the Doctor bit of his name. He began pushing the lever backwards and forwards and it creaked and huffed. "Bellows," he explained. "One of the greatest of the Roberts Brothers's inventions. Inside the hot air bag is a second bag. The second bag is filled with fresh air, which is heavier than hot air. So if I pump the bellows I fill the inside bag with fresh air. We get heavier and come down in a controlled landing. See?"

"No."

He began again, "Inside the hot air bag is a…"

"No. I mean I don't see how it helps us. We're still going to crash into one of the chimneys, be tipped out onto a roof and fall into the street," I moaned.

"No we're not," he said. "Trust me, I'm… an aeronaut!"

The balloon was falling faster now. We sped over the heads of men in canoes. They seemed to be wearing suits of animal skin and carrying bows and arrows.

"Those are the Wild People," Pa said. "Trying to stop supply ships getting in and out of the harbour."

I just nodded. I could see sailing ships at the quayside now, deserted and rotting in the water. Their tall masts reached up to snatch at us and bring us down onto their decks.

"But where are we going to land? In the river?"

"On the waterfront," Pa said calmly.

We grazed the tip of one ship's mast and it snapped off. The balloon basket tipped crazily and I held on to the costume box in the bottom. Pa began pumping faster now and we dropped even quicker.

People were gathering on the quayside and pointing up at us. I could hear their excited voices now. A horse screamed in fear and clattered off with the rider clinging to its neck. Rooks clattered, cawing into the air as we swept towards their roosts in the rooftops.

The window of a house opened and a woman in a blue checked dress looked out. I'll swear I could have reached out and shaken her hand.

We dropped down and brushed against the canopy of a grocer shop, bounced into the air and back down to the level of the ground-floor windows. Then we stopped. Suddenly.

Pa looked over the side. We were just above the ground – about head height to a tall man. The rope that held our wooden cannon had wrapped itself around the post of a gas lamp and it held us fast.

The balloon tugged and strained at the rope but it held fast. "Out, Nell!" Pa cried. "I told you I'd get us down safely."

I jumped out of the basket and placed my feet on the rope that was holding us. I did my tightrope walk down to the lamp-post, grabbed the post and slid down it.

The crowds of people who had rushed to get a closer view couldn't help but clap.

Pa just leaned over the side of the basket and dropped to the ground. He looked at me with some disgust. "Show-off," he muttered then turned and smiled suddenly at the crowd. "Ladies and gentlemen of Eden City," he cried. "Welcome to Doctor Dee's fabulous Carnival of Danger!"

The crowd clapped weakly, not sure just how they *should* greet a couple of strangers who dropped from the sky.

Pa turned to me quickly. "Suckers! Look at them. Hundreds of them. Suckers. We'll make a fortune then fly off!" He turned back to the crowd. "See Gregory the Great, all the way from Russia, fired from a cannon!"

"We left the net behind, Pa," I reminded him.

From the side of his mouth he muttered, "I'll fire you into the rigging of the ships! It shouldn't hurt."

"Thanks."

"See Miss Cobweb from England dance the tightrope," he cried.

"We don't have a tightrope."

"You just walked down one from the balloon... and see Captain Dare dive into flaming water."

"We don't have the pool with us," I said.

"Dive in the river."

"It's filthy!"

"We'll make enough money to pay for a bath," he argued.

At that moment there was a murmuring in the crowd and a small and weasel-faced man in a long black coat and blue dungarees pushed his way through. He had a silver star pinned to the coat and a brown moustache nearly as wide as his broad shoulders. "Sheriff Spade!" a woman in a dirty green shawl said to her friend with even dirtier, even greener teeth.

"Make way for Mayor Makepeace!" Sheriff Spade called.

A fat man in a fine black suit followed him and the crowd backed away leaving the fat mayor standing alone in front of us. "Welcome to Eden City!" he cried.

Now that was probably the last thing I expected to hear. We were used to being run out of town by angry lawmen who thought we were just there to rob Pa's suckers.[10]

"I see you bring us weapons for the fight against the Wild folk outside our troubled walls," the little mayor said. Even his voice was a squeaky weasel voice.

"We have?" Pa asked. It was unusual to see Pa lost for words.

The mayor nodded at the cannon.

"But we need far more than that. We need new muskets, gunpowder and bullets. We're getting desperately low."

The people in the crowd nodded gloomily.

"I'm sorry to hear that," Pa said.

10   All right, we WERE just there to rob the suckers. But they could take care of themselves. There was no need to call in the law. You could feel a LITTLE bit sorry for us travelling showpeople!

The sheriff stroked his moustache and squeaked in a voice like a flute, "The worst thing about the Wild Folk is that they don't just kill you… they *scalp* you! They take all your hair off by peeling the skin away from the top of your head. It's horrible."

"You've seen it?" I gasped.

"No, but I've heard the tales," the sheriff said and shuddered. "Brrrr!"

"But now you've come to our rescue!" the mayor laughed his full-bellied laugh.

"We have?" I asked.

"You and your flying machine can bring us in all the supplies we need," he said. "You can buy them in East River City and fly them across. Our ships are trapped in port by the canoe warriors."

I could almost hear Pa's brain ticking and his eyes darted round the crowd. "We'd need money to buy weapons," he said.

"We have all the money you need," the mayor said.

Pa's face split in a grin as wide as the Eden River. "That's a lot of money," he said and licked his lips.

The mayor waved a hand at a building behind him, round and squat as a toad. "Let's put you up at *The Storm Inn* for the night and you can set off tomorrow."

Pa put his arms around my shoulder and spoke from the corner of his mouth. "Of all the suckers in all the world, this just has to be the biggest little sucker of them all."

"Great," I sniffed. "Out of one disaster into another I'll bet."

FIVE

TROY – AROUND 4,000 YEARS AGO

Yes, back to where we started but time has moved on a little. Except for Achilles who was now dead. Death usually stops time moving on for most people. But Achilles was not "most" people…

Zeus sat on his cloud over the windy plains of Troy.[11] Hera smiled. This was rare. In fact Zeus couldn't remember the last time she'd smiled. "This is *much* more fun," she chuckled. (He *could* remember the last time she'd chuckled. It was when he'd sat on a thistle on Mount Olympus.)

---

11 Troy is famous for two things – a wooden donkey and the wind. Don't ask me why it's famous for the wind but it is. With this book you don't just get a story, you get a weather forecast too at no extra cost.

"Yes, Troy has been too boring for too long. That's why I got Paris to kill Achilles."

"And *now* you've had Paris killed!"

"Ah, yes," Zeus nodded. "Killed in a battle on the windy plains of Troy. Shot with a poisoned arrow and died very slowly."

"Why is it called the windy plain?" Hera asked.

"Dunno," Zeus shrugged. "Just one of those things. Troy has windy plains like…"

"… like Helen has a face that launched 600 ships," Hera put in.

"I thought it was a thousand ships," Zeus said.

"She's not *that* good," Hera sniffed.

"And she was no help at all when Paris was wounded. That's why he sent for his first wife, Oenone. She was a great healer."

Hera snorted. "Hah! Paris ran off with Helen and then expected his ex-wife to heal him! I'd have refused."

"Oh, Oenone refused," Zeus said. "She just let Paris die. Then, *after* he was dead she felt a bit ashamed and she killed herself."

"Stupid woman," Hera sneered. "Still, it's good to see *something* happening down there. We created these humans for our sport. It's good to see some action.

This siege is still pretty boring. Have you a plan to end it?"

"I have…" Zeus began. He stopped and looked up to the sun. His god-like ears heard the sound of beating wings somewhere higher than the highest clouds.[12]

"Ah!" Hera cried. "It's your wicked cousin Prometheus." The rare smile slid off her face like ice off a penguin's back.

The white-winged god slowed his flight, circled the cloud and landed gently beside the married gods. His face was tanned with the glare of countless billions of stars and he looked weary. He slipped the wings off his back and stretched.

"Good day, cousin," Zeus said. "Have you completed the task I set you? Have you found one true hero among those pathetic little humans?"

Prometheus (or Theus as we came to know him) nodded slowly. "I went forwards in time to search for a hero. I met some brave and bold people but never quite the perfect hero."

12 You will remember, if you were paying attention, that the gods had wonderful eyesight. I should have mentioned that they also had ears like bats… well, not pointy and hairy. I mean ears that could hear sounds that only bats (and gods) could hear.

"So you've failed?" Hera gloated.

"No," Theus frowned. "I've just not succeeded *yet*."

"You *failed*!" she cried.

"Not exactly…"

"So exactly what have you done?"

"I've been searching as Zeus told me and…"

"FAILED!"

Theus turned a little red in shame and looked down at the time-worn sandals on his feet. He shuffled them. "Ah, but…"

"Failed, failed, *failed*!"

"But, but…"

"There is no such thing as a human hero. Zeus set an impossible task," Hera spat.

"Did I?" her husband sighed. "Sorry, Theus."

"Gods can be heroes. Humans can't. They are too stupid and selfish," Hera explained.

Theus looked up, eyes gleaming. "You're wrong! I remembered Troy. There must be heroes at Troy!"

Hera turned sharply and said, "You had better hope you are right," she said with soft menace. "You know what will happen if you are wrong?"

Theus nodded miserably.

"Tell me what will happen, Theus?" she teased cruelly.

"You know," the demi-god mumbled.

"I know," she nodded. She licked her lips as if she could taste his torment. "If you *can't* find a hero then the Avenger will take you and destroy you. And it will serve you right. You deserve it for stealing fire from the gods and giving it to those creatures."

Zeus gave a small cough. "And the Avenger is on its way here now, Theus. I sent for it to take Achilles and Paris down to Hades in the Underworld. So tell me quickly if you can name a human hero and save yourself."

The demi-god took a deep breath. "Achilles?" Theus said.

"He's dead!" Hera spat.

"I arranged to have him killed last week. Anyway he was half-god," Zeus sighed.

"Paris, then?" Theus asked hopefully.

"He's dead too," Hera put in. "Clever Zeus had him done away with only yesterday. And he was a bit of a coward anyway! He was no hero." She rose to her feet and looked down on Theus with a look more poisoned than Paris's arrow. "No one – not even Zeus – can call off the Avenger. You're a fire-thief, Prometheus, and you will NEVER find a human hero because one has never been born yet."

"*Yet*," Theus nodded. He looked up at her and smiled gently. "Then I'll go back to the future and find one. There is a temple in a place called Eden City. The humans call it the Temple of the Hero. I found it when I went there in the year they called 1858."

Hera looked furious. "If this hero has a temple then he'll be dead. It doesn't *count*. You have to show Zeus a *live* hero."

Theus nodded. "I've thought of that. I'll go back to another year *before* he died. I'll find him and show him to Zeus *alive*."

Hera's mouth turned down at the corners as if she doubted the plan would work. But her eyes had a cunning glint in them. "And which human year will you go back to?" she asked.

Theus rubbed his star-worn eyes and thought. "I'll go back a human lifetime... they live for three score years and ten. Seventy years before 1858 is... er... 1795!"[13]

13 Oh, yes, YOU know the answer should have been 1788. But there was no school on Mount Olympus – the gods thought they knew everything. So Theus would have failed all the maths tests that you would pass. Don't feel sorry for him. He could fly beyond the furthest stars, which is much better than knowing how many tortoises make a dozen.

"So you will go to Eden City in 1795 will you?"

Theus nodded. Theus was a kind god who loved humans. He was brave and strong, honest, unselfish and loyal. He kept his fingernails clean and always washed behind his ears. He was just the sort of person you would want for a friend.

He could also be pretty stupid.

If you DID have him for a friend (as I did) then you'd have told him this: if you are on the run from someone who will grind you smaller than dust then you hide. And when you hide you do NOT tell anyone where to find you.

In a word, TRUST NOBODY.[14] Zeus jumped to his feet and the cloud swirled round his knees. "Wings," he said and he cupped a hand to his ear. "Flying fast as a shooting star. It's the Avenger, cousin Theus. Better flee!"

Theus gathered his wings and strapped them on quickly. He launched himself over the edge of the cloud and hid beneath it just as the Avenger landed next to Zeus.

Then Theus let himself drift gently down towards

14 All right, that's two words but you know what I mean.

Troy. The winds of the windy plains carried him silently out to sea. So silent that the Avenger couldn't hear him.

Once he was on the other side of the Earth he began to climb again. Beyond the clouds and past the moon. He left the planets behind and sped towards the stars. Out there time was different. If you could fly fast enough and leave the planets behind in a blur then you were racing ahead through time.

Theus was free and could have stayed there, safe for all time. But he missed those curious humans. He wanted to see Eden City again.

Zeus was in a good mood. He lay back on the cloud and looked at the feathered Avenger. Zeus could see it in all its ugliness. You couldn't. No human could see its true shape. When it was flying it looked like an eagle. When it was walking it looked like a hunched man in a feathered, golden cloak with a beaky nose and glittering eyes. Its neck was slightly twisted as if it had been broken once and never set properly.

"Well, Avenger, you seem to have failed to capture Prometheus," the god said.

The creature shifted from foot to foot, uncomfortable. "I will find him in time," it hissed.

"There's work to do at Troy first," Zeus said.

The Avenger sighed with a breath like the rattle of a rasp on hard wood. "Achilles? His body has been burned. Now I have to take his spirit to Hades in the Underworld, I suppose?"

"And Paris," Zeus said.

"Is he dead too?"

"Yesterday. Nasty accident with an arrow."

"Can't say I'm sorry," the creature said and shuffled. "I never liked the snivelling little coward."

Zeus pointed towards the massive walls of Troy. "See them? Their ghosts are wandering round the walls wondering where to go."

The Avenger stretched its wings. "Avenger dear!" Hera called. She smiled for the second time that day. "When you've done that small task then come back and see me, will you?"

The creature nodded stiffly then launched itself into a slow spiral glide towards the ghosts of Achilles and Paris.

They were arguing.

"… and I say it serves you right!" Achilles was raging. "It's not even as if you beat me in a fair fight. You had to hide under your sister's couch like… like a serpent. Then you wriggled out on your fat little belly."

Paris pouted. "My belly isn't fat."

"Not *now* it's not," Achilles agreed. "But it *was* when you were alive. I don't know what Helen saw in you. A woman so lovely her face could launch five hundred ships and she runs off with a weedy worm like you!"

"It was a *thousand* ships, *actually*," Paris shouted and the winds of the plains blew through him. "And you Greeks with your thousand ships *still* can't capture Troy. They never will."

"Want to bet?" Achilles said and he would have said it through clenched teeth if he'd had any. He jabbed a finger at his enemy's shoulder but it did no good. The ghostly finger passed through the ghostly shoulder and out the other side.

"Excuse me, gentlemen," a feathered figure interrupted. "Would you like to come with me?"

"You can see us?" Achilles said and he would have blinked if he'd had eyelids. "None of the others in the Greek camp or in the city can see us."

"I *know*," Paris groaned. "I went up to my ex-wife, Oenone, just as she was about to throw herself on my funeral fire, and I said to her, I said, 'Doesn't that jolly well serve you right?' I said. And do you know she acted like I wasn't there. I felt *such* a fool!"

"You are a fool," Achilles snarled and he'd have curled his lip if he'd had a lip.

"Now look here, Achilles…" Paris began.

The Avenger stepped between the two. "Paris. Shut up. I am taking you away with me and I don't want you squabbling like rats in a nest."

"Rats? It's years since I tasted a rat," Paris sighed.

But Achilles had other things on his mind. "Where are you taking us, feathered fiend?"

"I am taking you to the god Hades in the Underworld."

Paris would have rolled his eyes in horror if he'd had any eyes to roll. "Oh, hell!" he said.

"Exactly," the Avenger said and wrapped a wing round each dead warrior.

The ground seemed to open and a long stairway led down into the darkness of the dead.

Six

Eden City – 1795

You may remember we left my story at The Storm Inn
*on the waterfront of Eden City. Mayor Makepeace and the
people of that grim city seemed to think we were the answer
to their prayers. They were a city under siege – just like
Troy. Now, just like Troy, they had a Helen there to join
the fight. Me.*

Pa enjoyed himself that night. He sat in the bar-room
of *The Storm Inn* and told tales of his daring deeds. The
bar was crowded and it seemed everyone wanted to
buy Pa a drink. I sat quietly in a corner and sipped a
sarsaparilla. I'd spent an hour putting up our posters
around the town and it was thirsty work.

Now the terror of the balloon ride was over I felt

suddenly flat – a bit like the balloon really. And Pa's tales were all lies anyway.

"I was taught to fly by the Montgolfier Brothers themselves. The Carnival of Danger was performing in Paris and they came to see us. They wanted us to test their balloon for them. They'd sent up ducks and pigs but no human being had ever had the courage to go aloft. They turned to us."

An old and toothless man leaned forwards. "I saw your advert for that flying cannonball chap. I guess he went up…"

"Gregory the Great?" Pa laughed. "Greg wasn't so great that day. He doesn't mind being shot into a net but the truth is he is scared of heights. If he has to climb more than ten stairs to bed he gets a nosebleed!"

The crowd laughed. The old man with no teeth sucked his thumb. His wife had even fewer teeth and she said, "Stands to reason, you old buffoon," she sneered. "It's plain as the nose on an elephant's face – it must have been that Captain Dare! If he can dive into a flaming fire from a tall tower, he must have had the nerve to go up in that there balloon – got to be braver than some pesky performing pig," she said.

Her rubber lips sprayed everyone at the table with spittle when she tried to say 'pesky performing pig'. A lot of handkerchiefs wiped a lot of faces.

"Wrong!" Pa laughed and the old man gave his wife a nudge in the ribs as if his elbow was saying, 'Not so smart, are you?'

A man as thin as a scarecrow called, "Don't tell us it was that Miss Cobweb the tightrope walker? She'd be used to being up in the air. Don't tell us the first man in space was a woman?"

"Miss Cobweb did indeed offer to go up in the balloon," Pa nodded. There was a gasp from the audience and the scarecrow man looked pleased with himself. "But I could not let her take the risk. No, sir, there was only one hero with the courage, the nerve, the guts and the style to take on the mighty challenge…"

There was complete silence. You could have heard the beer drip off the dirty tables onto the sawdust on the floor below. Pa looked around. He held the moment as long as he could. Then he spoke in a low voice. "The first man to fly free was none other than… Doctor Dee himself!"

"Ooooh!" the crowd breathed as if they'd all been

holding their breath for 20 seconds – which they probably had.

The old man leaned forwards. "Who's he?"

Pa looked a little cross. "*Me*, of course. The magnificent Doctor Dee himself. You, sir, have the honour of buying the drink for the greatest aviator the world has known."

"You're an ape-y what?"

"A-vi-a-tor… a flier, a bird man."

"I haven't bought you a drink," the old man said.

"Then now is your chance!" Pa said and the audience laughed. The old man got to his feet and shuffled to the bar. He counted a few coins from a thin purse. His last coins by the look of it.

Pa looked at him as if to say, 'sucker'. Sometimes Pa's greed could make him crueller than a north wind in winter. I pushed through the crowd and pushed a bank note into the man's shrivelled hand. "Doctor Dee likes a joke – but he didn't really want you buying him a drink. Take this and get yourself and your wife one too."

He looked at me through watery eyes. "Why thanks, Miss…"

"Miss Cobweb," I told him.

"My name's Waters," he said. "Thank you, Miss Cobweb."

"It's a pleasure."

I went back to my sarsaparilla and another hour of Pa's tall tales. When a distant clock clanged midnight Sheriff Spade pushed the doors of the saloon open and called, "Right, folks, it's closing time. Get on home before I have to lock you all up!"

The crowd grumbled but rose with a clatter of chairs and stools and shuffled out into the night.

The sheriff walked up to Pa and spoke in a low, quick voice. "Listen, Doctor, as Sheriff I really should have the best musket money can buy. How much would that cost me?"

"Twenty dollars," Pa said quickly.

The sheriff smiled and pulled out a purse. "Is that all? I expected to pay twice as much!"

Pa almost choked on his beer. "Ah – oh – ooh!" he blustered. "You mean you want a quick-loading, flint-action, oak-butted Saracen Special?"

"I… I guess so."

"Then you are talking about sixty dollars," Pa said. The sheriff's face fell. "That much?"

Pa took the wallet from his hand and looked

through it. "You have fifty dollars here, eh? Tell you what," he said sliding the bank-notes out. "I may be able to do you a special deal – you being a lawman and all. I'll get you one for just fifty dollars. Don't tell everyone or they'll all want one!"

Sheriff Spade looked worried. "That would never do. *I* have to be the only man in town to have the best musket."

Pa wrapped an arm around the lawman's shoulder and guided him to the door. "Don't worry, Sheriff. I may lose a little money on the deal but I'll do it because I like you."

"You do?" the surprised Sheriff said.

"I do."

"No one else does!"

"They will when you own a Saracen quick-loader. They'll all look up to you." He placed a hand between the little man's shoulders and pushed him gently into the night. He tucked the money into an inside pocket. "Every one a sucker," he told me.

"Can you really get him a Saracen quick-loader that cheap?"

Pa screwed up his face in pain. "Ohhhh! Nell! You disappoint me. I thought you'd know me better than that." He held up a fist and counted off the plan on his fingers. "One, there is no such thing as a Saracen quick-loader. Two, once we get out of here we will not be coming back with a supply of guns. We will simply take the money and fly. If every sucker in town pays up as easy as the sheriff then we will make a fortune, Nell, a *fortune*."

Pa had pulled some pretty mean stunts in his time, but this was the biggest. "We'll never get away with it," I said.

"Trust me, I'm a doctor. We'll be rich."

I shook my head. "But these people are under siege. If the Wild Folk attack, and the people of Eden City have no guns, they could all be killed. You're not just robbing them. You're betraying them!" I argued.

Pa looked uncomfortable. "They don't need any more guns to hold off an army of men with stone axes and arrows. The Wild Folk will soon get tired of the siege and go away. They need to move to their winter camps to the south soon. You'll see. This is almost *too* easy," he smirked.

Of course *nothing* is *ever* that easy. There is always a catch. But I didn't know what it was till I rose from the flea-ridden mattress and left the damp *Storm Inn* bedroom next morning.

Fat Mayor Makepeace was sitting at a table with Pa chewing at some coarse bread and smelly cheese. "Eden City food isn't that good," the mayor was saying, "but once you're back with those guns we'll drive off the Wild Folk and live like lords. And *you*, Doctor Dee, will be treated like the greatest lord in the city – why, they may even put up a statue to you ... right behind mine!"

Pa smiled. "I look forwards to that," he said. "Now, do you have the order and the cash? Two hundred dollars should get you all the weapons the town needs." The weasel-faced mayor took out a scroll of paper and passed it across the table. "Will your balloon carry all these guns?"

"Sir," Pa said. "In tests in Rome this balloon lifted an elephant off the ground."

"I thought you said it was tested in Paris," the mayor reminded him.

"It was, dear sir, but we travelled all over Europe before we came to this far-flung continent," Pa lied.

The narrow eyes flickered quickly and the voice lowered to a mouse squeak. "Sorry, Doc, but I have to tell you there are one or two of the citizens of Eden City who… er… are a little worried."

Pa sat back in surprise and raised one eyebrow. "Worried?"

The mayor placed a heavy bag of cash on the table. "Worried that you may take the money, fly off and never come back."

Pa didn't even show a flicker of surprise that his plan had been discovered. "So… they want me to take you with us? There's no room in the basket. Not by the time we load all these guns," he added with a flick of his long fingers at the list.

"No, they don't want you to take me with you – you wouldn't get me up in one of those new-fangled monsters. No. They want you to leave the cannon behind."

Pa nodded. Suddenly the mayor turned his blob of a nose in my direction. "They also want you to leave the girl behind."

I gasped. "They can't do that, Pa!"

Pa held up a hand. "An insurance policy for you, a willing hostage, I'm sure we understand. Little Nell is the dearest thing to me in all the world… dearest apart from one thing…"

"One thing?" I asked.

"One thing?" the mayor echoed.

"One thing. My honour. If I leave Eden City, and promise to return, then all the Wild Folk in the world would not keep me from returning. My promise is stronger than the hardest steel. My word is as true as the aim on a Saracen rifle. I do not *need* to leave little Nell here."

The mayor chewed on a tough piece of bread and sucked on a grain that was stuck between his teeth. "The girl stays or the deal is off."

Pa spread his hands. "A thankless public is sharper than a serpent's tooth, as Will Shakespeare said."[15]

"Did he?"

"Almost. I am deeply hurt by your suspicion. But, when I think about it, it is better if I leave Nell here."

"Is it?" I cried.

"Why, yes. The less weight I have to carry, the more powder and bullets I can carry back from East River City. And as I *do* plan to return then you are not really a hostage at all!"

"I'm not?"

15 Pa had been an actor before I was born. He said being a showman was not much different.

"No, Nell, my dear. You need a little rest. A day or two in Eden City will do you no harm."

"But…" I began to object. Pa gave me a warning look and a small sign with his hand to stay quiet. "But… I'll miss you, Daddy dear!" I sniffled. (Pa wasn't the only one who could put on an act.)

"It won't be for long, dearly-beloved child. While I am in the sky looking down on East River City, then your dear mother will be up in heaven looking down on you! Protecting you while I am gone."

"She's not de…" I began to say, but gave a little choking cough and tried again. "She's not de-cided to join the angels and forgotten me?"

"A mother's love will never die," Pa sighed.

The mayor blew his nose with a grubby handkerchief then dabbed at a tear with the same stained rag. "A mother's love will never die. Did Shakespeare say that too?"

"No," Pa told him. "I did." He swept up the bag of money and smiled. "Good day, Mayor Makepeace. We leave in an hour."

The mayor rose slowly to his feet. "But the wind's still from the east. If you go up now you'll get blown *further* east. You'll get blown straight into the plains and the camp of the Wild People! We find, in these parts, the wind swings round to the west in the evening. Can you fly at night?"

Pa's eyes narrowed. "Even better," he said. "Even better. We leave tonight!"

"We?" the mayor asked and looked at me.

"Er… I mean *I* leave tonight!"

The mayor nodded and left us alone in the bar-room. I could see myself trapped, like that other Helen, in Troy and under siege. Well, not exactly like that other Helen – because I was prettier and she had had Paris for company. I would be all alone.

"Pa," I said. "You're not *really* going to leave me behind. Are you?"

"Don't be stupid, Nellie, of course I'm not."

"The name is Nell," I said.

SEVEN

THE UNDERWORLD – 4,000 YEARS AGO

I don't know what the Underworld is like. You have to be dead to go there.[16] *But I've heard the tales so you'll have to trust me when I tell you it is NOT the sort of place you would go for a picnic. It's not even the place you'd go on a school trip and they are usually bad enough. No, the Underworld of the gods was nastier than Mayor Makepeace's handkerchief.*

Achilles and Paris trudged down the gloomy corridors and the scent of death would have filled their nostrils… if they'd had nostrils.

---

16   Some smart reader is going to say, "Aha! There was ONE living man called Orpheus who went down to the Underworld to snatch his dead girlfriend back. In the end he failed and was torn into little pieces by a bunch of wild women." All right, I know about Orpheus. The point is I'm not Orpheus and MOST people are dead when they go there.

"I'm glad I haven't any nostrils," Paris muttered.

"Are you going to complain all the way to the Underworld?" Achilles asked.

"No. I'm just saying, this is not a pleasant place."

Achilles turned to him and glared fiercely. "We wouldn't BE here if it wasn't for your stupid little trick."

The Avenger stopped and turned. "I have warned you not to argue. You annoy me. And if I am annoyed I will tell the great god Hades of the Underworld to think of some new and nasty tortures for you."

Paris would have raised his eyebrows... if he'd had any.[17] "My dear old chum, Achilles. How nice it is to have you for company. Enemies in life but best of pals after death."

"Eh? Oh, yes! I look forwards to spending some time chatting about out lives at Troy. It was a tough battle, but it gave us heroes a chance to show the world what we're made of."

The Avenger hissed. "No need to overdo it."

---

17   Look, can I drop this "if he had any" stuff. They are ghosts. They have no bodies so they can't do the things humans do. But now you have the idea I can save my pen and ink and let you add "if he had any" in all the right places. Agreed? Good. Now I want to get back on the road to Hell. That's my intention.

It led the way down a path cut into warm rock. Warm but damp so it steamed a little. "Not long now to the Styx," it said.

"Oh, the Styx! That's where my mother dipped me when I was a baby," Achilles said.

"You have to pay Charon the ferryman one obol each to get across," their eagle-shaped guide told them.

"I don't have any money!" Achilles cried. "Money's no good on a battlefield."

"Don't worry," Paris told him. "I've got plenty. I had loads of loot in Troy. The trouble is there was nothing to spend it on. To be honest I'm glad to be out of the miserable place."

"It wasn't a lot of fun on the windy plains," Achilles said.

"What was it like?"

"Windy."

The Avenger made a grating sound that could have been a laugh. "Once you get to the Underworld you may change your minds. You may be begging to get back to Troy!"

The warriors stopped. "We're going to a land of heroes. The Islands of the Blessed, aren't we?" Paris asked.

The Avenger gave the laugh again. "Is that what you think?" It turned its glittering eyes on the ghosts. "When you cross the Styx you come to the Asphodel Fields. That's where ordinary humans wander around as ghosts. But you are NOT ordinary humans. You are killers!"

"Warriors!" Achilles objected.

"You will pass on to the next level of Hades and be taken to Tartarus. I'm sure Lord Hades will think of some suitable punishment for you!"

"Punishment? What sort of punishment?"

The hunched shoulders of the Avenger hunched a little more in a shrug as it walked on. "There's Tantalus down there. He is starving and thirsty. He stands in a lake up to his neck in water. But if he bends to drink the water dries up. He stands with the branch of a fruit tree over his head. If he tries to reach for the fruit then the branch is blown up out of his reach."

"Nasty," Paris muttered. "I don't like the sound of that. What did he do to deserve that?"

"He gave the food of the gods to the humans," the bird-shape sneered.

"Ah," Achilles nodded. "Just as Prometheus was punished for giving fire to the humans!"

The Avenger stopped sharply again. Now its voice was harsh as sharp steel on living bone. "Do NOT remind me of Prometheus. As soon as I've disposed of you two I will seek him out and destroy him totally. He will not escape. If it takes forever I will make him wish he had never been born. Hurry! Hurry! I want to get back on his scent!"

The ghosts hurried.

"I thought the Underworld was a pleasant place," Achilles grumbled.

"The people who lived good lives take the fork to the right and end up in the Elysian Fields – it's full of people dancing and singing," the Avenger explained. "Some people return from there to the world above – if they die and return to the Elysian Fields three times then they pass the rest of time in the Islands of the Blessed where sorrow is banished."

"I like the sound of that!" Paris cried. "Any chance we might get there?"

"Yes. Fat chance," the big bird spat. "Now here we are at the river Styx. Step into it."

A wide and lifeless river stretched out before them. It didn't glint and shimmer like an earthly river. Down here even the daylight was dead.

"I thought we had to pay to ride the ferry with Charon," Paris said. "I've got my obols ready."

"Step into the Styx and you will have new bodies when you step out. We cannot torture you if you don't have a body."

The bird spread its wings and the heroes fell backwards into the river of poison. They came up spluttering and swimming for their lives... or were they swimming for their deaths?

They struggled out onto the shore where the Avenger waited.

But the war heroes weren't looking at it. Their jaws dropped (now that they *had* jaws. Their eyes were fixed on the monster that stood in front of them next to the Avenger.

"What in Hell is that?" Paris breathed.

The creature was roughly human. But its body was almost square. It had to be. Along the top edge of the square sat its 50 heads. Down each side of its body were fifty arms.

The Avenger said, "Meet the Hecatonchires."

"Hello, lads!" the fifty heads called. That would have deafened the ears of the heroes but the air of the Underworld deadened even the loudest noise.

Paris waved a few fingers and said, "Hello, Hec!"

Achilles stood with his feet and arms apart like a wrestler ready to do battle with the monster. "I am the mighty Achilles. Come, monster, do your worst!"

"Ohh! Doesn't he talk funny?" head 35 said. The other heads agreed he talked very funny. "A bit like that Hector we had down here last month," head 3 said and again the other heads agreed. "Still you know what we say?" head 14 cried and all the heads joined in. "The bigger they come, the harder they fall!" and 50 heads laughed together while a hundred arms clapped the monster sides.

"Choose your weapon, creature from Hell!" Achilles cried and the heads giggled.

"Ohh! Creature from Hell, eh? Well sticks and stones may break my bones..." and the other heads joined in, "but names can never hurt me!"

Achilles turned purple with rage while Paris just looked a little worried. "Choose your weapon!" Achilles roared but his voice fell dead on dark rocks and pebbles at the edge of the poisoned river.

"Stones!" head 3 said. "We choose stones," and the third pair of arms waved at the stones by the shore.

Achilles swooped down and picked up a stone.

Then the Hecatonchires stretched down to its right and each of the fifty right hands grasped a stone.

But the weight was too much even for its massive legs. As the monster tried to straighten up it wobbled then toppled onto its side and the stones fell with a dull clatter to the shore. The Hecatonchires struggled to its feet. "Sorry, mate," head 35 said. "That always happens!" head 3 put in and the other heads said, "Always".

Paris stepped forwards. "Your trouble is you're not using your brain."

"*Brains!*" head 14 reminded him.

"*Brains*, then," Paris nodded with his single head. "You should lean to the right and pick up five stones, say. Then you lean to the left and pick up five stones in your left hands. Five at a time. Ten times to the left, ten to the right and you're fully loaded. That way you stay balanced, don't you?"

"I suppose he has a point there," head 35 said. "We can try it," 3 suggested. "Yes, try it," the others joined in.

At first it was a slow job rocking right then left.

"Left... two-three-four-five... and right... two-three-four-five!" it rocked. "Left... two-three-four-five… and right… two-three-four-oops!"

Paris clapped his hands happily. "It works!"

Achilles groaned. "You need to borrow one of the monster's brains because you seem to have lost yours?"

"I have? Why?"

Achilles just shook his head wearily.

Some stones were dropped. Head 17 swore a very nasty word that shocked the others. But after a while the monster got into a "left… two-three-four-five… and right… two-three-four-five!" rhythm and soon a hundred rocks were clutched in a hundred hands. "Righty-ho! Ready when you are," Hecatonchires head 35 said to Achilles. Achilles pulled back his arm and threw his rock. It smacked into the nose of 25 and the head roared.

A moment later a hundred Hecatonchires's rocks rained down on Achilles. His armour was crushed like a snail's shell under a horse's hoof. His new body was mangled and twisted, broken and battered. A blood-soaked head in a shredded helmet stuck out from the pile of stones. Paris removed a rock from Achilles mouth and his new teeth tinkled to the ground. "Are you all right?" the prince of Troy asked.

"Wa-waaaah? Waah-wah waaaah wah… wa-wah!" Achilles said in a spray of blood from broken lips.[18]

"I only asked," Paris said.

"Cor!" the Hecatonchires gasped with at least 40 of its heads. 35 said, "It works really well, doesn't it? Now we know how to load up we'll be unbeatable!"

Achilles body healed quickly – after all he was an immortal; he had a new body that could be hurt and bent out of shape but never destroyed. New teeth slid out of the empty gums and the flesh healed without a scar. He pushed off the heap of stones and rose shakily to his mended legs. "If we'd had a creature like that at Troy we'd have won in ten minutes, not over ten years."

"Just as well you didn't," Paris laughed.

Achilles glared at him through his even-newer eyes and was about to hiss something through his even newer teeth. But he stopped. He grabbed Paris by the arm and dragged him away from the Avenger. He whispered so low, not even the eagle-ears of the bird caught the hero's words. "We can't stay in this awful place. I've a plan to get us out of here. Just back me up

18   Of course you don't need me to tell you what that means. You do? Very well, it means, "All RIGHT? What do you think, dummy?"

and agree with me… no matter how odd it sounds."

"Yes," Paris nodded.

"Yes what?"

"Yes, I'm agreeing with you. You told me to."

Achilles wondered if his old enemy would make a very useful friend, but he turned to the Avenger anyway. "Avenger!"

"What is it Achilles? I'm in a hurry."

"I know. You want to get after that evil Prometheus."

"That's my business."

"No! It's everyone's business. You can't have a dangerous demi-god like that on the loose," Achilles said.

"I agree," Paris said.

"That's why the gods have an Avenger like me," the bird snapped and clacked its beak.

"And you are treated so badly by the gods. They send you out to do an impossible task. Even if you find Theus you'll struggle to hold him on your own."

The Avenger felt its twisted neck and knew it was true. "Perhaps," it said.

"You need a couple of true heroes to help you."

"I do," the bird said. "Zeus expects me to do

everything. Chase Prometheus through space and time then stop to take heroes to Hades."

"It's SO unfair," Achilles sighed. "I wouldn't blame you if you got a bit of expert help."

"Pah! There is no expert like me," the Avenger said and its beak lifted proudly in the air.

"I agree, but a couple of heroes would be useful... someone like me and Paris."

"Yes, I could use a couple of good men..." the Avenger nodded.

"And a monster," head 17 of the Hecatonchires put in. "Especially now I've learned how to throw a hundred rocks at the same time!"

The Avenger almost had a smile on its beak. "I promised Zeus I'd take you to Hades, Achilles... but I didn't say *when*. After we've caught Prometheus I can always bring you back here, can't I?"

"You could," Achilles said carefully and shook his head at Paris who was going to say, "Not if I can help it!"

"But Zeus would never give me the extra wings you'd need," the Avenger sighed.

"His wife Hera might," Achilles said. "She doesn't like Paris much, but she likes me."

The Avenger's savage eyes looked deep into Achilles's eyes. "I'll take you with me," it said.

"And me?" Paris said.

"And me?" head 35 asked.

"Yes. Together we will capture the Fire Thief and I will destroy him! Destroy him!"

Prometheus had reached the farthest stars again and time had tocked forwards enough. He headed for Eden City in 1795.

EIGHT

EDEN CITY – 1795, THE DAY AFTER WE ARRIVED

Have you ever had this really creepy feeling that things keep happening to you? Things that you have no control over? As if someone was pushing you around like a piece on a chessboard? The way things came together that day seemed normal at the time. But, looking back, I can see a weird "Fate" was making things happen. So, if you don't believe in Fate you won't believe what happened next. Take this book back to the shop or library. Get your money back. Do NOT read on!

Prometheus drifted down on his wide white wings towards the ugly smudge by the river that was Eden City.

He'd been here once before, in the future.[19] Then

the city had been covered by a cloud of purple and yellow, green and brown, grey and black. Twisting towers and sharp spires had risen out of the mists.

Now, in 1795, the city was smaller and a wooden wall had been built around it to cut it off from the living plains of waving grass. Eden City stood there like a dark wart on a beautiful face.

The buildings were not so high in those days but they were rotting and dank, the streets dark and snaking and puddled and muddied.

Theus hung in the air and saw a bright flash of yellow flame explode below him. Then there was a hiss and a lump of lead flew through his arm.

The (half-)godly ears heard a man far below cheer, "I got it! I hit that big bird! It'll feed the family for a week! I got it!" Theus saw it was an old man as twisted as an Eden City street.

A sour-faced old woman cackled, "Fool! If you hit it then why hasn't it fallen? You couldn't hit a barn if

19   Yes, I know that doesn't seem to make sense. You can go to a place that you've been to in the PAST but not to a place that you've been to in the FUTURE. But Theus was a time traveller. He had been to Eden City in 1858 when it was even grimier and uglier than it was when I was there. Sounds unlikely, I know. But I have lived so long, and I am so old! We're ALL time travellers – it's just that most of us move forwards. Theus could move both ways.

you were standing inside it. You've just wasted precious powder and shot we could have used against the Wild Folk!"

"I was sure I hit him," the man sighed and moved back towards the shabby shack the couple called home.

"Why don't you do something useful?" the woman demanded. "Go out and rob some poor stranger."

"If they're poor they're not worth robbing!" the old man grumbled.

"You *know* what I mean. Now you go out stealing. I have to get back to the baby farm."

Theus shuddered. He'd given these humans fire. They used it to make choking smoke. They'd learned to use it to kill. "It was never meant to be like this," he sighed and rubbed his wounded arm. It was already beginning to heal. "Maybe Zeus was right. Maybe the humans are too simple to be given fire. Maybe it's right that I should be punished for it."

Even a great demi-god can get gloomy from time to time.

Theus looked down at the people hurrying below. Mostly he could see bent backs as the Eden City citizens looked down at their feet to make sure they didn't step into something too disgusting. Only the bird-hunter had been looking up.

There was one girl that Theus spotted who didn't hurry. She seemed to be wandering around like some stranger. Her hair was reddish-brown and her face lovely enough to launch a thousand ships. In fact she was the loveliest girl you could wish to see in Eden City... ever. [20]

I was drifting through the streets, just passing the time till it grew dark and it was time to leave. Pa had told me he would NOT be leaving me behind. He said he had a plan... but he would tell me at supper.

To stop me moaning he sent me out to prepare our escape. "We need a clear space in this crowded city to lay out the balloon ready to fill it with smoke. And then we need at least one strong man to carry the balloon along to that clear space. Off you go."

"What will you be doing?" I asked him.

"Resting... I need to be awake tonight if I'm going to fly the balloon back over the river to East River

20   Yes, all right, so this beautiful girl was ME. I know you'll think I am telling a small lie here but I never saw a prettier girl in Eden City in the time I was there. No, honest, I REALLY didn't. I can tell you don't believe me, but I don't care.

City." Then he climbed the stairs to his *Storm Inn* bedroom and left me to explore the city alone.

No one smiled or said hello to a stranger in Eden City. No one smiled full stop. The windows of the houses and shops were clouded with grime. I'm a curious sort of person – I like to see the way people live. So I wandered the streets peering in to the grimy windows.

The shops had little food – because of the siege, I guessed. And the clothes gathered dust on the rails as Eden City people were too mean to buy new ones.

Horses and the odd cart rumbled past and you had to jump out of the way. The wooden sidewalks creaked and tripped you. I thought that was why Eden City people walked with their heads down but looked quickly from side to side.

I suppose I was wrong. There was another reason why they looked around nervously as if their lives depended on it. The reason was… their lives depended on it. But I was a stranger. I wasn't to know.

I passed one house that looked dirtier than the rest and wondered what went on inside.

The front was as faded and dirty as the rest of the houses. But this one had a bright new red sign on the door. In yellow-gold letters it said, "Mrs Waters' wonderful world for children. The nicest nursery in town".

I squinted through the window. The bare wooden floor was covered in cradles. Some were so still the spiders had woven their webs around them like some Sleeping Beauty bed.

A woman sat and looked at one cradle and rocked it. One child whimpered and another coughed. But the round-shouldered, grey-shawled, stick-thin woman ignored them. Her eyes were fixed on the one baby. She spooned some milk from a cup and fed it to the baby with a cooing sound.

She seemed to sense my eyes on her back and turned round with a face that was axe-sharp, axe-hard. It was a face I'd seen in *The Storm Inn* the night before.

I moved away quickly down the dull street, past the dim alleyways, looking for somewhere wide enough to take our balloon. But I was looking ahead. I wasn't looking down the alleys. That's when I found out why the people of Eden City looked from side to side all the time.

There was danger in the darkness, even in the

daylight dimness thieves lurked. One waited till I'd passed the murky opening then stepped out behind me. His hard hand wrapped itself round my throat and dragged me back into the passage between two windowless walls. "Give me your money or I'll cut your throat."

It was an old, twisted hand on an old and twisted man.

I've been in rough towns before and Pa taught me how to deal with people like this. "Let go of my throat or you'll choke me and never get my money," I croaked. He loosened his grip but held on to my jacket. I turned to look at him. It was the toothless old man I'd bought a drink for last night at *The Storm Inn*. I'd felt sorry for him!

Pa's advice was, 'Confuse the suckers'.

"Have you got any change?" I asked.

"You what?"

"I don't have any change. I just have bank notes. Tell me how much you want and let's see if you have the change."

"Why… I have fifty cents," he said.

"Show me."

He struggled to hold my jacket in one hand and

fumbled in his pocket with the other. He pulled out some change and showed it to me.

I picked out half of the coins.

"Now, I have no change at all. So add nothing to 50 cents and you have 50 cents. Half of fifty is 25, yes?"

"Yes."

"I take 25 cents and leave you 25 cents. We both have 25 cents and everyone is happy!"

"Ye-es!" he said and frowned and let go of my jacket.

You won't believe what happened next.[21]

There was a rustle of feathers and a huge shape dropped from the grey sky into the greyer alleyway. A man with white wings strapped to his back landed behind the old robber. He was a large young man with skin the colour of bronze and muscles as smooth and swollen as our balloon.

His face was as handsome as my face is beautiful. His hair was a little too long and girly but no one is perfect. He reached forwards and picked up the

---

21   But I'll tell you anyway. You want to know, don't you? Or maybe you want to guess. Go on. Guess. I made a run for it? Nope. He saw he'd been tricked and called out "Stop thief!"? Nope. See, you'll have to see what I was going to tell you anyway.

robber by the collar of his ragged jacket. "I saw him trying to rob you," the stranger said. He was dressed in a light tunic with no sleeves and no trousers. Must have been cold, I thought.

I suppose you'd have fallen to the floor in a faint. What would that get you? Muddy clothes.

I'd been weird places and seen weirder sights in our travels. It wasn't long since I'd dropped out of the sky myself. So I guess I wasn't as shocked as I should have been. I may have blinked… once.

"How did you see us?" I asked.

"I was flying over the city," he explained.

"On those wings?" I asked.

"There's no other way to fly," he said.

"I use a balloon myself," I said.

"A what?"

"We use fire to make smoke and lift a big bag in the air," I told him.

His face brightened. "Ah, so you humans have found one good use for fire. I'm pleased."

"I'm pleased you're pleased – but will you put the old man down before you choke him to death?" I pleaded.

He dropped the thief into the damp dust. The old

man staggered and looked lost. He looked at us. "Been nice meeting you," he said and smiled his toothless smile. He jingled the coins in his hand. "My wife will be pleased with this 25 cents," he said with a dazed and glazed look in his eyes as he wandered, wobbling into the main street.

"I'm Theus," the large stranger said.

"I'm Helen," I said and held out a hand to shake.

I'll swear his bronze skin turned a lot paler when I said that.

"Who?"

"Helen. Never heard the name before?"

"Oh, yes," he murmured. "But that was in Troy."

"Is that beyond East River City?" I asked.

"Way beyond," he said.

"Look. My pa is looking for a strong man to help us. Want to come back to *The Storm Inn* with me?" I offered. Then I looked around me. "If I can find my way back. This city is like a maze – a maze made of water that shifts every time you move."

He nodded. "Eden City is like a living thing," he agreed. "You should have seen it when it grew bigger in 1858!"

"Eh?"

"Never mind. *The Storm Inn* is this way," he said, pointing the opposite direction I'd have gone. At the time I guessed he'd seen *The Storm Inn* when he was flying over.

He slipped his wings off and tucked them under his powerful arms then set off towards the waterfront district.

I followed.

NINE

ANCIENT TROY – 4,000 YEARS AGO...
BUT LATER THAN LAST TIME WE WERE THERE

Now you see how the different parts of the story are coming together? If I were a fiction writer then that's just the way I'd make it happen. But, of course, I'm not a fiction writer because this story is true. I'm telling you what happened to me over sixty years ago. But the tale of the Avenger, the Heroes and the Hecatonchires hasn't come together with Theus and me – yet. Be patient, dear reader. Be patient!

Zeus had gone down to the windy plains again. He was disguised as a wise old Greek and he was going to meet the Greek leader Agamemnon. He'd told Hera of his plan.

"I'm going to persuade the Greeks to build a huge,

hollow horse made of wood and standing on wheels. They are going to fill it with soldiers and leave it on the plain," he said. "The Trojans will take the wooden horse into the city and the Greeks rush out to massacre the lot of them."

"It'll be a bit windy, won't it?" Hera argued. She could see a clever idea coming along and she was annoyed. Why hadn't she thought of it? Zeus would be *so-o* pleased with himself if the idea came off. He would boast about it for the next ten years.

"The Greeks will be nice and snug inside that horse, believe me," Zeus said.

"No they won't," Hera sneered. "Those humans use something we gods don't need," she reminded her husband. "Something called a toilet. And if they don't use the toilet it can get very, *very* smelly inside a horse."

Zeus was annoyed at this fault in his plan. "They'll just have to go before they get into the horse."

Hera the sneerer gave a little snort. "Carry on. Tell me why the Trojans would take this wooden wonder into their city?"

"The rest of the Greeks... the ones NOT inside the horse... will get into their ships and sail away.

The Trojans will think they've given up and gone home. They will open the gates and take the wooden horse inside the city!" he cried.

"Why should they?"

"Because they will believe it is a holy Greek statue. They will take it as a prize of war," he said.

"No they won't. If they see a big wooden horse they'll say, 'Ooh! Look! A big wooden horse!' Nobody in Troy will think it's a holy Greek statue," she scoffed. "No one will think of wheeling it into the city."

Zeus wriggled on the cloud over the city. "You could be right," he said.

"Zeus, I am *always* right. It's a daft plan."

Zeus became angry and reached into a pouch on his belt and pulled out a thunderbolt. He threw it down to Earth in anger – and set fire to three Greek tents. The wind whipped the flames and singed the beards of the scattering, screaming soldiers. "Oops!" Zeus said. Then he turned to his wife and said. "Look, we are bored with this war. Have you got a better idea to end it?"

Hera gave a small smile. "I'm glad you asked me that. I have. You go to the Greeks and tell them to build a huge, hollow horse made of wood and standing on wheels. They fill it with soldiers. The Trojans wheel it in to the city."

She paused. Zeus glared at her.

She smirked. Zeus glared at her.

"Go on," she said. "Ask me."

"No."

"Go on. You want to know."

Silence. Suddenly Zeus snatched a thunderbolt and hurled it at Troy. A few of the topless towers lost their tops.[22]

Zeus spoke quickly like a sulky child. "Oh very well then you great-minded, great-mouthed goddess and tell me *why* the Trojans will wheel the horse into the city."

Hera placed her hands calmly into her lap. "Because a spy called Sinon will go into Troy and *tell* the Trojans that this horse is a holy Greek statue. Sinon will *tell* the Trojans that it is a gift of peace from the Greeks who've gone home."

"And you think they'll believe it?" Zeus asked.

---

22 Oh, go on, argue. How can a tower with no top lose something it hasn't got. That's what you're going to say. I know it. Well, listen. It was a famous playwright from England called Christopher Marlowe who said Troy had "topless towers". He meant they were incredibly high and the tops were lost in the clouds. See? Now let's get on.

"They will."

"So where do I find this Sinon chap?"

Hera shook her godly head. "No, Zeus. *You* simply disguise yourself as Sinon. It's easy for you to slip into the city and spread the word."

Zeus jumped to his feet and said, "I'll go and do it right now."

"Aren't you forgetting something?"

"Am I?"

"First you have to visit the Greek camp and get them to build the horse. It's only *after* the horse is built, and the Greek ships have *left*, that Sinon should go to Troy."

"Yes… I knew that," Zeus lied. "When I said I'll do it right now I meant I'd visit the Greeks with the horse idea."

The god smoothly changed his shape into that of a wise old Greek teacher and drifted down from the cloud to the edge of the Greek camp. A guard spotted him. "What is the password, stranger?" the guard called out.

"Let me through or I will push a thunderbolt down your throat and roast you from the inside out," Zeus snarled.

The guard scratched his head. "That's not the

password they told me."

"What did they tell you?" Zeus asked.

"They said the password was *windy*."

Zeus clapped his hands. "Well done, soldier. That is correct. The password is *windy*. You have passed the test. I will tell your general Ulysses what a good guard you are," the god said as he walked into the camp.

The guard turned red with pleasure. "Why, thank you, sir. Thank you."

Later that day, as the sun set, Zeus was leaving Ulysses after explaining the trick with a wooden horse. "And you think it will work?" Ulysses asked looking up at the half-finished statue tall as the walls of Troy. The men were working on through the night by the light of bonfires that were whipped into sparks by the wind from the sea.

"It will work… just so long as you tell your men to go to the toilet before they get inside the horse," Zeus said.

As Zeus crossed the plains he wished he could just fly into Troy. He didn't do a lot of walking – gods don't. His feet began to hurt and he kept stepping on rusting swords, shattered armour and squidgy body-bits that the burial troops had left behind. A battlefield can be a messy place. A ten-year-old battlefield can also be a very smelly place.

Ashes blew in his face from the funeral fire that had been built to burn the corpse of the hero Achilles. Zeus gave a grim smile as he brushed the ashes off his tunic. "You'll be tucked away in Tartarus by now, Achilles," he muttered and walked on towards the mighty walls of Troy. He headed for one of the secret gates that was so secret everyone else had forgotten about it.

Night was falling and Troy was in darkness.[23] But Zeus had the eyes of a god and could see his way clearly through the stone-paved streets and up to the palace of King Priam.

Behind the shutters of the darkened windows his sharp ears could hear sharper voices complaining. "Mum, I want a drink of water!"

"Shut up and get to sleep or Hector's ghost will

23 "Aha!" you cry. "Of course it was in darkness if it was night!" But I mean there were no candles or torches lighting the windows in the houses, streets or topless towers. Candles are made from fat, and fat is precious food in a starving city. The candles had all been eaten. Trojans went to bed early and left the streets in moonlight – that's because they couldn't eat the moon though they would like to. They believed it was made of cheese!

come and get you!"

"But Mum, I can't get to sleep. All that hammering is keeping me awake! What is it, Mum?"

"The Greeks on the windy plain are building something."

"What they building, Mum? Ladders to get in?"

"No. Mrs Palamon next door says it's a big wooden model. Looks like it's going to be a dog."

"Cor! Mum! Can I go on the walls tomorrow and have a look."

"Only if you go to sleep now."

"Cor, Mum! The Wooden Hound of Troy! That'll go down in history that will!"

"Sleep! Now!"

"Night, Mum."

"Nighty-night. Mind the bugs don't bite."

"They tried, Mum, but I ate them. Night!"

"Night!"

Zeus walked on. He could hear the hammering too. But even his godly ears missed the soft grating sound of rocks sliding apart. A gateway from the underworld opened on the plain near the ashes of Achilles.

Hera, on the cloud over Troy, could see the gateway

in the thin moonlight and the sparks from the Greek camp fires. First an eagle head on a twisted neck appeared and looked around carefully. The enormous bird-man stepped onto the sandy plain and made a sign for someone below to follow.

Achilles stepped into the silver light and then Paris. Finally a creature with fifty heads used a hundred arms to pull itself above ground. The gateway slid shut.

"Urgh!" Achilles gasped.

"Shh!" fifty-two mouths hissed at him.

"But I just stepped in these ashes!" the hero complained.

"They're cold," Paris said. "They wouldn't hurt."

"No… but they are the ashes of MY body!"

"Urgh!" Paris nodded.

"Shh!" fifty-two mouths hissed at him.

"Now wait here and keep quiet," the Avenger said.

"Shh!" fifty-two mouths hissed at him.

The creature clacked its beak, annoyed. "We don't want anyone to know Achilles and Paris are back on Earth. Hera wants to see me. Wait here and I'll be back before dawn. Then we set off in search of Prometheus."

Fifty-two heads nodded.

The eagle spread its wings and softly clattered into the air letting the dusty wind lift it towards the curious cloud.

Achilles nodded towards the walls. "There are a lot of guards on the walls tonight."

"They're looking at us, I think," Paris said.

"We need to get them to keep their heads down," Achilles said.

"Leave it to me," the fifty-headed monster said softly.

The Hecatonchires wandered round the plain looking for rocks and building them into two piles to each side of its square body. Then it began to pick them up with a little chant, "Five to the left – five to the right – five to the left – five to the right!" until its hands were full. "Hey! I didn't fall over!" head 35 grinned.

Achilles squinted towards the Greek camp and the hammering. The fires lit up a monstrous wooden statue. "They're building a wooden cow!" he exclaimed.

"Shh!" fifty-one mouths hissed at him.

"No, lads. That's what the people on the walls of

Troy are looking at. They can't see us in the moon-shadows. They're looking at the pig!"

"The wooden swine of Troy," Paris said. "I wonder what that's all about."

"Never mind, it means you can drop those stones, Hec!" Achilles ordered.

"Aw! Do I *have* to?" head 17 moaned.

"Just drop them anywhere."

"Seems a shame to waste them," head 3 said. The monster wound back fifty pairs of arms and threw them at the walls. Trojans screamed in panic as a storm of stones hit them and the tops of the walls crumbled. They staggered home, bruised and bleeding, not sure what had happened out there in the darkness. High above them the Avenger settled next to Hera and she had already called Hermes the messenger. The young man was complaining. "Dragged me out of my bed you did! I didn't know I was supposed to be a 24-hour delivery service! It's not fair. Nobody else has to come flying when you click your fingers. I'm going to complain to Zeus when I see him."

Hera sighed. "Hermes, just fetch three pairs of wings from Olympus and do it before dawn. Our friends must be off the plain before sunrise."

"Puh!" Hermes pouted and flew off with a buzz of feathers at his winged feet.

"Thank you," the Avenger said. "I will find Prometheus no matter how long it takes."

Hera smiled and her teeth shone in the moonlight. "Oh, it won't take very long at all," she said.

"He could be anywhere. When that god dies he gives off a green spark. I have to search the Earth through time, looking for it."

"No you don't," Hera said, teasing. "Not if someone told you exactly where to look and when."

The Avenger spread its wings and its eyes burned so fiercely they washed the dark streets of Troy with a red glow. "You know?"

Hera spread her hands. "Just go to Eden City. Eden City in the year the humans will call 1795."

"Yes-s-s-s!" the bird hissed so loud even the hammering horse-builders stopped in wonder.

TEN

EDEN CITY – 1795

Now you may be worried that Theus would be grabbed by the Avenger and destroyed. Can you just stop worrying about him and think about ME for a change? I was going to be abandoned in this ugly city by my own pa, remember. Left as a hostage. Yes, we know Pa said he had a plan to get us away but Pa made a living from lying. Would YOU trust him?

Theus led the way to *The Storm Inn*. He seemed to know the city well and the twisting lanes that confused me were no trouble to him.

"You've been here before?" I asked.

"Yes, in 1858," he said. "The city was even bigger then… I mean it *will be* even bigger then. Dirtier and smokier," he said. "Just on this corner there'll be a factory owned by a Mr Mucklethrift and it'll vomit out purple smoke all day long till you choke on it even when you're a mile high."

I was sure then that I'd escaped from an old thief and fallen into the clutches of a young madman.

We passed the balloon that lay on the quayside limp as a dead cat – yes, a red-and-white striped cat perhaps but lifeless now the hot breath of life had gone out.

Theus nodded. "Yes, I could carry that," he said.

I stopped suddenly. "I said I'd go out and look for a place to launch the balloon. We need quite a wide space without the buildings around. The quayside's just too narrow. We could drop into the water if we don't get it right."

Theus nodded. "We need to go to the prison, then."

"Uh?"

"There's an open space in front of the prison – about the only open space in Eden City," he explained. "It's big enough to take five thousand people. They go there to watch."

"Watch what?"

"Prisoners being hanged," he explained.

"Nice."

"No, it's not nice at all. I was hanged there in 1858," he said.

"Mad," I muttered. I reached into the basket of the balloon and pulled out some costumes. There was a red suit with white stripes that Pa used to wear sometimes. I found a black shirt and black hat to go with it. "We need to dress you in these or people will think you're a bit odd," I said.

"I know," Theus nodded. We waited for a cart to rattle past too fast and crossed the road to *The Storm Inn*.

There was a stage where singers and actors performed on a Saturday night. It was dark and quiet now. The red curtains were dusty and mottled. "Go behind there and change," I said. I went behind the bar, into the kitchen and found us a large meat pie to eat and a jar of ale.

The kitchen table was as dirty as the bar-room floor but the pie was fresh. I left my 25 cents on the table top to pay for the food and carried it back to the bar-room.

The suit was a little tight on Theus but he looked good in it.

"I left my wings under the stage," he explained. "I may need them if the Avenger arrives suddenly."

I shook my head. "Look, Theus, we don't leave till

this evening. Have some pie and ale and tell me your story."

That's what he did for the next couple of hours. I would repeat it now but it would fill a book.[24]

Dusk came early to Eden City. Even without that Mucklethrift factory there was a dirty haze that hung over the city and blotted out everything but the midday sun.

Pa came down looking full of life after his long rest. He looked at Theus. "Perfect," he said. Theus described the square in front of the prison. "Perfect," Pa said. He peered at Theus in the gloom of the room. "I have a suit like that!" he laughed. "I use it for my fire-eating act."

"You eat fire?" Prometheus gasped. "I didn't give fire to the humans to eat," he mumbled.

That puzzled me but Pa didn't seem to hear.

"It's all a trick, my boy. I don't really eat it, you know. In fact I could show you how I do it…"

"Pa!" I cut in. "We need to work out how I'm

---

24 Theus reckoned someone will be writing that book after 1858. So if you are reading THIS after 1858 there's a chance you'll find that first book. He reckoned it would be called *The Fire Thief* or something like that. But it's not my job to sell books for other writers! If you CAN'T find *The Fire Thief* then just buy another copy of THIS book. I need the money.

going to escape from Eden City. The mayor and the sheriff want me to stay behind as a hostage."

Pa sat at the table, poured himself some of the ale and supped at it. He pulled a face. "Cloudier than the Eden City sky and nearly as sour as your ma!" he said.

"The plan!" I said.

"It's foolproof," he said. And he told us what it was. Theus was sent out to buy a net from one of the fishermen on the waterfront and he stowed it in the balloon. I was given money to buy straw from the stables next to the inn and wool from the clothes shop on the corner. Theus went back out to buy a rope and rig it across the prison square.

It was fully dark by the time the landlord of *The Storm Inn* came downstairs and opened the bar to the public. But people hadn't come to buy his bitter ale. They'd come to see the famous aeronaut – the man who was going to bring them guns and set them free (they thought).

The sheriff put a hand on my shoulder. "Stay close to me, little lady," he said.

"My name is Nell, not little lady," I said. "And I'm as tall as you!" He looked surprised at my anger. I think he was worried I might be more trouble than he had imagined. He jangled the handcuffs on his belt. My being chained up would ruin Pa's plan. I had to learn to keep my temper.

There were crowds outside the inn and they helped Theus carry the balloon and the basket to the prison square. Our wooden cannon was roped to the basket and trundled along behind.

The people of Eden City led the way carrying lanterns that glowed yellow as well as many lights they'd taken from the idle ships that were coloured red and green.

It was almost like a party procession. The pickpockets had the best of the party, of course, but no one could get near the bag of money Mayor Makepeace carried with an armed guard.

Pa's plan meant the crowd, the mayor and the sheriff had to be distracted. He was going to give them a bit of a show so they'd forget about little Nell, their hostage. Sadly Pa forgot a couple of things, too ... but you'll soon find out what they were.

The balloon was placed in the square on the cobbles and the fire-box filled with the straw. Pa could have lit it with his tinder-box but instead he took a long wax taper and lit that.

"And now," he roared above the noise of the

jostling crowd. "Now I will light the flame that will heat the air and make the balloon rise."

There was polite clapping and the crowd fell silent. They expected him to place the taper in the straw – instead he placed it to his mouth. He blew. A ball of fire shot out and lit a thousand startled faces.

Theus turned to a couple of children and said, "I gave that fire to humans, you know!" The children edged away from him and ran to cling to their mother's skirts. Can you blame them?

There were cheers. Pa did that a couple of more times before he blew his ball of flame into the fire-box and set the straw alight. I hurried across and piled the woollen material on top of the blazing straw. "My assistant Nell is making smoke," Pa declared. "It is the smoke that makes the balloon rise."[25]

Theus stepped forwards and held the balloon bag over the smoke, as Pa had told him to, so the bag was filled. "It will take ten to fifteen minutes to fill," Pa told the crowd. "In the meantime Miss Cobweb

25 YOU know it is hot air that rises. YOU know that it isn't smoke that makes a hot air balloon lift off the ground. But you have to remember these were the first days of balloon flight. In those days the aeronauts believed it was smoke that let them fly. So, of course, Pa and I believed it too. It's in the history books if you don't believe me.

from England will perform on the tightrope!"

Four men were given the job of holding the fishing net under the rope in case I fell.

"Ooh!" the crowd cried as I climbed a drainpipe at the side of a house and hoisted myself onto a rope that stretched across the square. I was supposed to give one or two slips to make the crowd gasp. (Really they wanted me to fall – not because they hated me but because it would be more exciting.)

But that night my slips were real enough. I was nervous about Pa's plan – and the wind was whipping over the water from East River City. For some reason that upset me but I didn't have the time to work out why. Anyway, Pa should have worked it out for himself but HE forgot. (And, by the way YOU should have worked it out too by now!)

I staggered to the far side of the square and was glad to slide down the drainpipe to the solid, filthy cobbles. I ran to the balloon basket. It was filling quickly now and starting to strain on the ropes. "Hey!" Sheriff Spade called. "You aren't going to escape that easy. You stay here till Doctor Dee gets back with the guns!"

He grabbed my arm. "No," I hissed. "I'm just going to change into my Captain Dare costume," I told him.

"I can't escape unless I'm in the basket at the same time as Doctor Dee and the money."

He nodded. "That'll never happen," he said grimly and let me climb in to change. The balloon above my head was tight now and the ropes straining. The next two minutes would bring us escape... or disaster.

I was changed and out of the basket in a minute. Pa was calling, "... and as I rise into the air my friend Captain Dare will thrill you all by flying out of the cannon. I want you men with the net to stand by the prison wall. If Captain Dare misses he will smash into the ground or be splattered against the prison wall!"

"Ooh," the crowd gasped. Half a minute to go. As I climbed into the mouth of the cannon, Pa climbed into the basket of the balloon. I looked towards the back of the cannon where Theus stood. "Best of luck, Theus," I said. "I hope you find your hero and escape from the Avenger."

"Thank you, Helen of Eden," he said with that handsome grin. "I will."

I let myself slip back into the darkness of the barrel.

As Pa shook hands with the mayor and took the cash bag, Theus stood with the lighted taper at the back of the cannon.

Quarter of a minute to go. "Untie the balloon!" Pa cried. It was tied to a metal ring set in the prison wall – probably the place where they chained prisoners. Someone untied it and the balloon jumped upwards.

Theus took a rope that was fastened round the mouth of the cannon and wrapped it around his wrist. That would hold the cannon steady and give a better aim. A loose cannon could skid across the cobbles when it went off and I could end up anywhere. I didn't want to end up anywhere. I was aiming for one place… and it wasn't the net tonight.

Five seconds.

"Freedom for Eden City!" Pa yelled and the crowd cheered.

Theus pulled hard on the rope. From inside the barrel I felt the cannon tip upwards.

Two seconds. I looked out and didn't see the net – I saw the balloon basket.

One second. Theus lit the fuse.

Whap! The spring sent me out of the barrel like a bullet and I soared into the air. Pa stretched out his arms over the side of the balloon basket to catch me.

What a pity he forgot those two things!

ELEVEN

*Sorry. I have to leave my story there with me hanging in
the air between a balloon and a crowd that would tear me
apart if I fell into their greedy clutches. Writers call that sort
of ending a "cliff-hanger" where our heroine is left hanging
on the edge of a cliff. Will she survive, you wonder? You
have to read on, don't you, to find out. Very irritating.
I wasn't even hanging on a cliff edge – I was hanging onto
the air between life and death. But we HAVE to get back
to Greece.*

Hermes was in a better mood when he arrived back
at Troy with the wings for the hunters. He circled over
the Greek camp where the evening fires were dying

down now. They were beads of light, strung out like a glittering necklace. The sea beyond was midnight blue, the setting moon was thin as a sickle and the stars burned gold and green. The sky was turning the faintest shade of grey-pink in the east as dawn was just a while away.

It was a very peaceful scene in the middle of this tiresome war – only the endless hammering of the Greek carpenters shook the early-morning air. But Hermes was content.

Even the monstrous fifty-headed Hecatonchires down below him looked like a soft, stuffed toy.

Hermes landed gently and placed the wings on the dusty earth in the shadow of the walls. "So what are you up to?" he asked the heroes.

The Avenger turned its savage beak on the messenger. "Mind your own business!"

Hermes's mouth fell open. His good mood vanished. "Well, there's gratitude for you. I'm dragged out of my bed to run errands for you and that's the thanks I get."

The Avenger stepped towards the god with wings on his ankles and hissed, "When I have destroyed Prometheus I may just come back and destroy you,

Hermes, you idle, vain and stupid little god."

"You can't do that! I haven't done anything wrong!" the god squeaked but didn't sound too sure.

"I'll think of something," the Avenger said in a breath as soft as the camp fire flames and just as deadly. It turned away to collect the wings and pass them to its deadly new gang.

"Zeus would never let you! You're a big bully bird, that's what you are! I'm going to tell Zeus you've been picking on me – threatening me. You'll be sorry."

The Avenger went still as the Trojan wall. Then it turned very slowly back to Hermes.

"Oop!" Hermes gave a little hiccup of fear.

A long wing stretched out and wrapped itself around Hermes's shoulder. The messenger shivered. "Oop! Don't hurt me!"

Now the Avenger's voice was soft as a spider's web. "Sorry, Hermes."

"What?"

"I shouldn't have threatened you. I am so-o glad you gave up your sleep to help me. There's no need to tell Zeus about my little outburst of temper, is there?"

"What? Oop!"

"We are on a secret mission to capture Prometheus

and we don't want our secret to get out. But I can trust you, can't I?"

"Yes. What? Oooop! Ahhhh!" Hermes had a sly look in his eyes. "You don't want Zeus to know what you're up to, do you?"

The Avenger tried to smile but it's hard to smile when your mouth is a beak.[26] "It was Zeus that sent me to punish Prometheus," it said.

Hermes blew out his lips, "Prrrr! But Zeus has changed his mind. He thinks Theus has suffered enough. He would call you off if he could."

"He can't!"

"But he *could* if Theus performs a task. That's why he said Prometheus can go free if he finds a human hero."

Bony spurs on the Avenger's wing went tight around Hermes's shoulder. "Not if I get Theus first," it said.

Hermes wriggled then stopped. His hiccups had gone. "Ooh!" he breathed. "*I* know what you're afraid of. Zeus ordered you to take Achilles and Paris to Hades. He doesn't know you've set them free to help you. He certainly doesn't know you've let that

---

26 It's true, isn't it? When did you last see a greenfinch giggle, a sparrow snigger, a blue-tit titter or an albatross go tee-hee? Gannets don't grin and seagulls don't smirk because they can't. Sometimes it's a sad life being a bird.

grotesque monster from Hell loose too."

"Here!" head number 35 of the Hecatonchires objected. "Watch who you're calling go-pest."

"Yeah," head 17 nodded. "Our mum says we were gorgeous when we were a baby! What does go-pest mean anyway?"

The Avenger pulled Hermes away from the others and said, "We fliers have to stick together, Hermes... mate."

"Mate? No one's ever called me that before. The other young gods are jealous of my wings, you know."

"Oh, I know. I have the same problem. So, when I get back, you and I will have to make sure we're the best of friends. *Do* things together!"

"Things?"

"Go for a flight somewhere nice."

"Where?"

"The seaside."

"Great!" Hermes cried, happy again. "Can we build sandcastles?"

"I'll call for you at Olympus as soon as I get back," the Avenger said.

"Promise?"

"Promise."

Hermes shook his head. "Funny, isn't it? Theus is hunting a hero. You're hunting Theus and Zeus would be hunting you if he knew about these three!"

"Sandcastles," the Avenger said gently.

Hermes's ankle-wings whirred and he lifted happily into the night air as the Avenger waved. When the messenger had gone beyond the clouds the Avenger growled, "Bird-brain!"

It turned to its three helpers. "Get the wings strapped on. We need to be away from here before Zeus gets back from inside Troy. We've a long journey ahead of us."

By the time the dawn sun blazed through the eastern hills, the colour of blood, the Avengers, two heroes and the monster were flying towards it.

The bravest of the Trojan guards lifted their heads over the walls. One was thin as a topless tower. The other was fat as a barrel... which was odd in this starving city. "That rock-thrower's gone. We're safe," the thin one sighed.

"And that Greek statue looks finished. I told you it was a squirrel! The wooden squirrel of Troy," his fat friend said.

"It's a horse – the wooden horse of Troy," a voice said. The guards turned and saw an old man with a white beard standing behind them. "How do you know, old man?"

"Call me Sinon," the shrunken figure said.

"How do you know, Simon?"

"Si-*non*!"

"Sorry, Si-*non*."

"I was a spy in the Greek camp. I heard them plan it. After Achilles died they were very upset. Most of them said they wanted to go home. Then *Paris* died and others agreed – they'd killed the man they'd come to kill," Sinon said.

"Makes sense," the tall, thin guard said.

"I *thought* they came to get Helen – they're not going to go back without the wife they came for," the barrel-bodied guard argued. "Not after ten years of trying."

"Ah," Sinon said. "They have their own wives back home in Greece. It's time to quit. Look!"

As the blood-red sun brightened to a fiery orange the guards saw the tattered tents begin to come down.

More guards joined them on the wall that overlooked the sea. Then a trickle of Trojan people climbed the walls to watch as word got around, "The Greeks are going!"

"Without Helen?"

"Looks like it. See? They're heading for the ships!"

"Aw! I'll miss them!"

"You *what*? Are you mad? We're free."

"Suppose so."

By the time the sun was white and hot as steel it seemed everyone in Troy was crowding onto the wall. "They've gone without me," Helen sighed. "I didn't think they'd ever leave without me."

King Priam shook his head. "Your face wouldn't launch four hundred ships these days."

"Thanks," Helen said bitterly. "No husband Menelaus, no boyfriend Paris and hundreds of miles from home."

She watched as the sails of the Greek ships were raised and the fleet headed over the horizon. By afternoon there wasn't a Greek to be seen.

"Open the gates of Troy!" King Priam ordered.

The order was echoed around the ancient city, "Open the gates of Troy!"

It rang around the city, voice to voice. Crier to crier.

Then the answer rang back. "Where are the keys? Where are the keys? Where are the keys?"

King Priam blushed. "Well, of course, I am the king and the keeper of the keys."

"So where are they, sire?"

"I… er… don't remember. It's ten years since I last needed them. I can't remember where I put them. Sorry!"

Zeus (in the body of Sinon) looked towards the wooden horse and wondered how the Greek soldiers were managing without a toilet inside. Something had to be done soon or the whole plan would be ruined. He stepped forwards. "Allow me, sire. In my youth I was an expert with locks."

"You were a lock-smith?"

"No. A burglar. But I am sure I can open the gates of Troy," he said.

"Give it a try, old man, and I'll be in your debt for life. I'll even let you marry Helen."

"No thanks."

Zeus-Sinon walked down from the walls and looked at the lock. He blinked and looked again. He blinked again and looked again. He looked up to the king. "The gates aren't locked, sire," he called.

"What? We've kept the Greeks out for ten years and nobody noticed that we'd forgotten to lock the gates? Oooops!" the king laughed. "Better not put that in the history books or we'll look right chuckleheads!

Ah, well, open the gates of Troy!"

Sinon turned the handle and the gates swung open for the first time in ten years. The wind from the plain swept in and blew away the stench of a dying city. It was like air rushing in to a lung. It was like wine to the trapped people of Troy and they drank in the sea-salt air.

Strangers hugged one another in the street. Helen appeared from the palace to see what the fuss was about. The crowds who had hated her gave her a cheer. A woman, drunk on the powerful air, jumped into the fountain in the weedy town square and called, "Three cheers for Helen of Sparta!"

"Nay, Helen of Troy!" someone shouted back.

"Helen of Troy she is! The face that launched three hundred ships! Hip! Hip…"

"It was a thousand," Helen said but her protests were swallowed in the wild cheers.

Sinon ran back up the stairs to the ramparts of the city wall. He ran too fast for an old man but no one seemed to notice. "King Priam… you *must* get that wooden horse into the city. Put it in the city square. Let the people have a party with lots of wine."

"We will."

"But *soon*, sire. It's a big statue and it will take all

afternoon to move it. We have to have it in the city tonight," Sinon urged him.

"Why?"

"Because… it looks like rain!" Sinon said.

Priam squinted at the sky. Only one cloud in sight. "It hasn't rained for weeks!"

Zeus waved up at the cloud and saw Hera listening. She nodded and waved her hands till she made a whirlwind that sucked up the sea into a cloud of slate grey that was ten times larger than Troy.

The shadow darkened the day. King Priam ran along the ramparts. "I want a hundred men to bring that horse inside. A hundred men and I want them now! Hurry! We don't want our precious gift to get wet!"

Men and women ran out with ropes and fastened them round the legs of the wooden horse.

It was like a party game. They pulled and heaved till it started to roll. They marched faster and faster till some of them were trotting along. They began to sing in time to their steps. The horse jolted and creaked through the open gates and rolled to rest in the city square.

The people turned to Priam for praise. He looked down and ordered, "Turn off the water to the fountain!"

"What?" the thin guard gasped.

"And let the fountain flow with wine!"

"Wine? We haven't had wine for ten years," the fat guard sighed.

"Ah… yes… no… there may be a few hundred barrels in my palace cellars," Priam said and blushed.

"You miserable monarch," the fat guard cried. "You kept it all for yourself?"

"I didn't drink it," Priam pouted. "Well, not with *every* meal."

"Hah!" the fat guard growled and went off to help fill the fountain.

It was just like a party game. And every part game has to have a prize. The prize for capturing the Trojan Horse was the greatest prize of all.

And its name was death.[27]

27 Don't worry. As we leave Troy I can tell you that not everyone died. That night the soldiers slipped from the bowels of the wooden horse and let in the Greeks who had sailed back. They only killed the men and boys – who would miss them? The girls and women were turned into slaves – which can be quite pleasant if you stay cheerful. And Helen? She was sent back to miserable Menelaus… which served her right. Her face would never launch another ship.

TWELVE

Remember where you left me? Fired from a cannon up into the air. Shooting towards the waiting arms of my father. But did he catch me? "He must have done," you say. "Otherwise you wouldn't have been here telling us this story now," you say. If you say that then you are not quite as witless as you look. But you have to remember I wasn't safe yet – I did tell you there were TWO things Pa forgot to do. Maybe you haven't worked out what the two things were? I suppose you want me to tell you? Oh, all right...

As I sped up into the cool night air I saw Pa's grinning face ahead of me and his large hands grabbed me by the wrists.

A moment later he'd pulled me over the side into the basket. "Ha!" he roared. "I *told* you to trust me! We have the money *and* you're free."

I staggered to my feet and looked at the prison wall as we climbed past it. I tugged off my false moustache and looked back down.

The crowd was slow to take in what they'd seen. But Sheriff Spade wasn't. "My hostage! My hostage is getting away. I never lost a hostage in my life and I'm not losing one now. Grab that man!"

Now that sounded a little odd to me. What was the use telling people to grab Pa when Pa was sailing over their heads and out of their reach. And the other odd thing was that the sheriff wasn't really pointing at Pa. He was pointing at something below the basket.

I leaned over the side as far as I dared and looked under the basket. That's when I saw Pa's first forgetting.

He'd forgotten to untie the cannon from the basket.[28] We reached the end of the rope and felt the

28 Yes, of course you spotted that, so you're sitting there smug as a mouse in a cheese factory. You are saying, "Ohh? Why didn't YOU remember, Nell?" Well, mouse-face, I had a lot of other things to worry about – things like missing the balloon and ending like a swatted fly on the jailhouse wall.

balloon's climb suddenly slow. Pa looked over the side. Not only was the cannon hanging on the end but Theus had the cannon rope wrapped round his wrist and it was pulled tight. He was being lifted too.

With the cannon and Theus pulling us down the balloon just didn't have enough smoke to sail into the clouds.

Sheriff Spade was one of the first to act. He jumped up to catch the dangling legs of Theus... but he was too short.

"Stop that man! I never lost a hostage yet and I'm not gonna lose this one!"

The basket bumped against the prison wall and hung there. Pa and I were just about level with the top of the wall and could look down on the other side. Pale prisoners in grey rags looked up at us in wonder. Pa waved. "Just passing!" he called to them.

But if someone grabbed our god's legs then we'd be 'just passing' on the way back down.

"More wool on the burner, Nell," Pa ordered and I climbed to the side of the basket to obey.

A few of the Eden City people tried to help the sheriff but it's hard to look up and walk straight. A lot of them fell over one another into a pile on the cobbled square. A tall, thin man was our biggest danger. "Grab those legs, Mike Pike," the sheriff ordered. Mr Pike looked up… and tripped up. He fell over an old lady's stick and knocked it away. She fell to the cobbles and Mike Pike fell on top of her.

"That's my wife you're assaulting!" an old man cried and began to beat the thin man with his stick. Someone dragged the old man away but a younger woman started to kick at him. "Leave my pa alone, you bully!" she screamed. She kicked out but hit a boy in the backside. His mother slapped her face and in moments twenty men and women were brawling, battling and bruising each other under the basket. Only the sheriff kept his eyes on Theus and the dangling legs.

Then the sheriff had a great idea. "Get to the top of the prison wall and drag that couple out of the basket," he ordered.

"To the top of the prison wall," the mayor roared over the top of the screams of the fighting women.

"To the top of the wall!" went the cry. Ten men rushed to the gates of the prison and collided with it.

"The gate's locked, sheriff," one man shouted.

Sheriff Spade shook his fist wildly. "Locked?

Locked? Locked? Why is the prison gate locked?"

"To keep the prisoners in. I guess," someone told him.

"Unlock the gates," the sheriff ordered.

"The prisoners'll get away," someone cried and a ripple of panic ran through the crowd.

"But if we don't get inside, my *hostage* will get away," the sheriff moaned and hammered on the door with his pistol.

Looking down on the hats and the upturned faces I could see both sides of the prison gates. "Who's there?" a guard called from the inside.

The smoke from the balloon rose thickly and the balloon edged up the wall with a grating sound. The sheriff looked up in panic. "It's the sheriff."

"How do I know?"

"Know what?"

"Know you're the sheriff," the guard said.

I waved at the guard. "It's NOT!" I called down. "It's a jail-breaking friend of Mad Dog McGrue!"

"Ooh! No! Help! We're being raided by Mad Dog McGrue's friends!" the guard wailed.

"No you're not!" the sheriff cried.

"Yes you are," I said as the balloon climbed an inch higher.

"You shut up!" the sheriff called to me.

"Help! Mad Dog McGrue's partner told me to shut up," the guard sobbed.

"I did NOT," the sheriff shouted.

"He did not," I agreed. I had to do some quick thinking. "He said 'shoot up'. He meant he's going to shoot up the gates if you don't set Mad Dog McGrue free."

"No! No! No!" the guard said and waved his hands as if he was attacked by a swarm of mad wasps. He looked up at me. "What can I DO?"

"Fetch Mad Dog McGrue to the gates. Then if the man outside shoots at the gates he'll shoot his friend!"

"Yes! Great idea. I will! I will! I will," the guard told me and ran into the prison. The crowd outside had worn themselves out with fighting and some staggered to lean on the prison walls, some slumped to the ground.

Theus hung by his trapped wrist patiently. When you've spent 200 years chained to a rock then you must learn patience. When you've had your liver ripped out every day for those two hundred years then an aching arm won't seem like much to suffer.

The sheriff squinted up at me and called, "If Mad

Dog McGrue makes his escape then he'll bring terror to Eden City. It will be all your fault."

The crowd turned their grubby and greasy faces towards me. "No it won't," I laughed.

"Why not?" the mayor put in.

"Because there's no such person as Mad Dog McGrue. I just made him up."

"You did?"

"I did."

"Why?"

"To buy us some time while the smoke builds up," I told him.

The balloon swelled and inched up again. The mayor shook a fist angrily. "That is a VERY dangerous sort of man to invent, young lady. If you are going to invent make-believe friends then invent a little puppy or a fairy – but NOT a mad gunman who could scare the poor people of Eden City into nightmares!"

"Sorry," I said. The guard ran back to the gate. We were creeping clear of the top on the prison wall now but someone could easily grab the cannon or Theus and haul us back.

The guard shouted through the gate. "The governor won't let Mad Dog McGrue out… but he says you can come in…"

"Then open the gate," the sheriff ordered.

"But you can only come in if you have a letter from the sheriff," the guard said.

"I AM the sheriff," the sheriff screamed.

"The governor said you have to prove it by giving me a letter from the sheriff," the guard went on.

I have heard of people tearing out their hair in a rage but I'd never seen it till then as the sheriff threw his hat to the ground and grabbed his hair in both hands.[29]

"Give me some paper, someone," he begged the crowd. Someone ran off to find a piece while the cannon climbed above the wall and only the legs of Theus could be caught now.

The sheriff scribbled a note with a quill, paper bag and ink-pot that a grocer brought him. We were almost too high to catch now. The figures below were getting smaller and I could hardly hear them.

"Here's the note from the sheriff," the sheriff said.

"I can't see it," the guard told him.

29 This may hurt you, if you ever try it. But not so much as it hurt Sheriff Spade. He'd forgotten he was holding a heavy pistol in his right hand when he threw his fists to his head. Crunch. Ouch.

"Open the gate and I'll show you."

"I can't do that. The prisoners'll get away," the guard said. "You'll have to bring a note from the sheriff if you want me to open the gates and read your note from the sheriff."

The last I saw of the sheriff he was on his knees, sobbing and banging his head against the gates.

"Are you all right, Theus?" I called down.

"Don't worry about me," Theus said and gave a smile as if he made this sort of trip every day of his life.

I stoked up the grate with more straw and the blaze made the balloon glow like a red-and-white striped moon. We were sailing on air. Higher over the prison now. The twisted streets became like a tangle of dark wool and the river ran its oily way to the west.

To the east there was the blackness of the plains and the mountains. Small camp fires of the Wild Folk twinkled, warm and welcoming.

That was when I realized Pa had made a second mistake.

Of course someone as clever as you will have spotted that one too. So you don't need me to tell you what it was.

There may be one or two sad and simple readers who DON'T know what he'd done wrong. But I'm afraid *they* will have to wait a little while to find out what clever readers like you already know...

THIRTEEN

SOMEWHERE OVER THE RAINBOW

It is almost the moment you have been waiting for. The time when my and Theus's story joins with the Avenger's. But not quite yet. Because Theus was hanging from our balloon. He wasn't where Hera had said he was… in Eden City. So the gruesome gang were close… but you get no prizes for being close.

The Avenger flew through space and through time. The Hecatonchires flapped on behind. Sometimes the heads chatted to one another. Sometimes they chatted to Achilles and Paris.

"There are lots of moons out here," head 7 said.

"I've heard the Earth's moon is made of green cheese," head 17 said.

"I like cheese," head 41 put in. "Can we stop for a bite?"

"Yes, why not?" head 37 agreed.

"Just going for a light lunch," head 35 called to Achilles and Paris. "We'll catch you up later!"

The Hecatonchires dived towards the green moon of the planet Soz and landed in a small village and a family rushed out to see the stranger.

The man and wife, the young boy and his older sister all had fifty heads and a hundred arms.

The Hecatonchires waved a hundred hands but soared on over the village to land in a field.

"They looked friendly enough," head 17 grinned.

"Should we stop and say hello?" 11 asked.

49 heads turned red as a sunset. "Too shy," they muttered.

The Hecatonchires picked up some Soz soil and head 22 tasted it. "What's it like?" head 35 asked.

"Soil," head 22 sighed.

"Not cheese?"

"Not cheese."

"Better get on with the flight, then," head 43 said.

The godly wings flapped and the Hecatonchires lifted into the air. "It was a funny sort of planet," head 47 told the others.

"Funny? The people all looked just like us!" head 35 argued. "Not like Earth where those funny humans have 49 heads and 98 arms missing!"

"Nah," 47 insisted. "Some people on this planet were ODD... they had long hair!"

"No! That was a girl."

"I've never met a girl before," head 37 sighed.

"She was pretty, wasn't she?" number 16 said. Forty-nine heads agreed.

The Hecatonchires flew off into star-spotted space. That brief, cheese-seeking landing was soon forgotten by the Sozpeople.

But one Sozgirl smiled fondly as the Hecatonchires flew away. "He was handsome, wasn't he?" head 16 said. Forty-nine heads agreed.

The Hecatonchires joined the others. When the Avenger's gang reached the farthest star they turned right – because that was the way to move forwards in time. The Avenger swung round and led them back to Earth the way a goose leads its flock in a "V" shape.

Earth appeared and the group swept to the dark side where Eden City smouldered like a piece of rotting seaweed on a hot night.

Paris wrinkled his fine nose as they dropped to the top of the purple clouds. "It smells worse than the Hecatonchires!" he sniffed.

Achilles flew alongside him. "You have the stomach of a sickly kitten," he sneered.

"No! I'll swear I've smelled that somewhere before. In the temple. When the priests make a sacrifice to Zeus."

Achilles shrugged. "Burning mutton?"

"No. Sometimes the priests get lazy and just throw the whole sheep on the sacrifice fire," Paris said.

"Burning wool? You can smell burning wool?"

"Yes!" Paris said, excited. "Maybe there's a temple here where the lazy priests are making a sacrifice to Zeus... look out!"

He added the last two words because suddenly a huge red-and-white striped ball loomed up out of the cloud ahead of them. It had some strange writing on the side that the heroes didn't understand... even if they'd had time to read it. The Avenger swooped easily round the side of the monster ball while the Hecatonchires bobbed up and fifty heads screamed "Wheeee!" at the same time.

Two humans were sitting in a basket below the ball

but they were too dazzled by the flames from the burning straw and wool to see the four fantastic fliers in the midnight sky.

A rope dangled over the edge of the basket and something was weighing the rope down. But whatever was there was hidden in the thick cloud.

The Avenger dived down towards Eden City and slowed. People were trudging wearily along the streets and seemed to be making their way home. One or two carried flares made from twisted twigs and the flames reflected in the eyes of the robbers who hid in the alleyways. Some of the men carried muskets and headed for the city walls.

The Avenger signalled for its three helpers to stay in the air till all was quiet.

When the last light dimmed in the last house, and the city settled into oily darkness, the Avenger led them down to the waterfront. Paris and Achilles landed softly on the quayside beside the hunched shadow of the Avenger. The Hecatonchires managed to clumsily snap off the mast of a ship whose mast was already broken. It scattered empty lobster pots across the quay then tangled its two legs in a pile of fishing nets. "Oooops," heads 21, 36 and 43 cried together.

A frightened dog barked at them then scuttered away into an alley at the side of *The Storm Inn* to hide and try to forget the nightmare it had just seen.

The Avenger ordered the Hecatonchires to hide below the deck of the abandoned ship with the broken mast. It passed the wings of the heroes down into the ship's hold and ordered the monster to guard them. Achilles and Paris fell asleep on the coarse heap of nets and left the Avenger alone with its thoughts. They were dark thoughts. Thoughts of chains and rocks. Thoughts of revenge and raw liver. It crossed the road to *The Storm Inn*. The place was asleep. The snoring of twenty travellers shook the shutters. The bird–like beast couldn't scent that a Titan god had been inside. Maybe tomorrow morning it would go in and ask some questions. If Theus was back in Eden City then *The Storm Inn* would be the place he'd go.

The Storm Inn… or the Temple of the Hero. The bird shuffled along the deserted streets, trying to remember the way to the Temple. It plodded past a house with a sign saying, "Mrs Waters' wonderful world for children. The nicest nursery in town".

Babies coughed and mewled weakly behind the

cobwebbed windows. The Avenger paused a moment and looked in to see a round-shouldered old woman lit by a weak and smoky candle. "I'm busy, Mrs Waters. So very busy. But one day I may be back for you to take you straight to Hades. One day."

The old woman looked up from the cradle where she sat with a stump of mutton-fat candle and spooned food into the mouth of a dark-haired baby. She shivered and warmed her hands at the candle. "Brrrr! I think someone just walked over my grave," she cackled.

It was truer than she thought.

The Avenger shuffled on, its claws scratching along the wooden sidewalks. A faded sign said, "*To the Temple of the Hero*".

The street was a dark shadow. The lane that led to the temple was a shadow of a shadow. Darker than the Underworld of Hades. The Avenger stepped into the inky air.

There was a soft swish in the air and a blade brushed against its feathered throat. "Your money or your life?" an old man's voice creaked in the coal-cellar blackness.

"My life," the Avenger whispered.

"Eh? You're not supposed to say that."

"So sorry to disappoint you," the Avenger breathed. With a swift move of the head it had the blade in its beak. A moment later a crunch of the beak shattered the steel blade.

"That cost me fifty cents!" the old man complained. He wore a very dirty handkerchief over the bottom half of his face. He lifted it angrily. "I'll report you to Sheriff Spade, I will! I need that knife to make my living. That's a tool of my trade, that is. I'm the Phantom of the Night…"

"The what?"

"Phantom of the Night. I'm famous in Eden City I am. The Masked Marauder, they call me."

"I thought they called you Phantom of the Night?"

"At night they do. In the daytime they call me the Masked Marauder. Anyway, I could have the law on you! You owe me sixty cents."

"I thought you said it cost you fifty cents."

"The price has gone up since I bought that knife. In fact you can't *get* them any more. You've ruined my life," the old man said and his pale eyes glowed in the dark street.

The Avenger had met many angry people but had

never met this problem before. "I'm… sorry," it stammered. Then it snapped its beak shut and shook its feathered head. "No I'm not. You tried to *rob* me! You're a *thief*!"

"Even a thief has his rights," the old man said. "I have a right to be paid for the damage you did to my knife."

"No you *don't*!"

"Then let's see what Sheriff Spade has to say, shall we?"

The Avenger was foaming at the beak with rage. "Listen carefully. I am going to kill you and take your spirit straight to Hades if you don't do as I say."

"No need to be like that," the old man huffed.

"I AM like that. It's MY job to be like that. So close your toothless mouth and listen…"

"Hah! You're a fine one to talk about being toothless," the man grumbled.

The Avenger ignored him. "Listen, Mr Waters. I will spare your life if you can help me."

"How do you know my real name? I am the Phantom of the Night!"

"I know more than you think," the beak hissed. "The one thing I do not know is where my prey is."

"If you want to pray you can go to the Temple…"

"Prey, I said. The man I am seeking. His name is Prometheus."

"Never heard of him."

"No, but you may have *seen* him. He is tall compared to you miserable humans. He has long, dark hair and golden skin. You would probably call him handsome. He has white wings and flies."

"He has flies? So does the rubbish dump at the end of our street," the old man said.

The Avenger gave a grating sigh. "I *mean* he has the power of flight."

"Ah! You mean Doctor Dee!"

"Do I?"

"A showman in a top hat. He flies. He has a young daughter that walks on ropes."

"No, no, that doesn't sound like him. Prometheus would look like a young man to you."

"Well, you could be talking about Doctor Dee's assistant. He wears a red-and-white striped suit. Very strong."

"That sounds like him," the Avenger said and his claws clacked on the cobbles as he shifted his feet, excited. "Where can I find him?"

"Oh, he escaped earlier tonight. Got caught in the balloon and flew off."

"Balloon?"

"Big bag of hot air. They have a sack full of money they tricked the people of Eden City out of. I hate them."

"Because they tricked you?"

"No, because it's such a great idea. I wish I'd thought of it," Mr Waters, the Phantom of the Night, sighed. "I'd be rich now, I wouldn't have to wander the streets phantoming people, would I? I mean, it's bad for my old feet is this marauding all day then phantoming all night. It's a killer!"

"So am I, Mr Waters," the bird breathed. "But you have been useful to me so I am going to let you go free."

"What about my knife?"

The bird blinked and leaned towards the old man. Its sour breath made his watery eyes stream. "Knife? I am giving you your *life*. Now tell me, where did they fly to in this baboon?"

"Balloon."

"Baboon, balloon… who cares? Just tell me where they were headed?"

"That's the strange thing!" the old man gasped and wiped his nose on the handkerchief around his face. "They flew off to the west... they headed for the country of the Wild Folk! They'll lose their scalps! They're as good as dead!"

FOURTEEN

THE PLAINS OF EDEN CITY – 1795

It sends a chill through your body, doesn't it? Imagine going to a hairdresser for a hair cut. He slips a stone knife under the front of your hair and pulls backwards. Whoosh! You'll never need a hair cut again! I wonder what would happen to a bald man? Would they scalp him anyway and use the scalp to patch the elbows in their shirts? It was one thing I never got to ask the Wild Folk. Anyway, they weren't the scalping savages we imagined, which was just as well...

You'll have spotted Pa's second "forgetting" before I did. I was just so *pleased* to have escaped from Eden City I didn't think of where we were going. We climbed through a cloud and three or four gigantic birds rushed past us and made the balloon shake.

Pa fell to one side and grabbed a rope. It was just bad luck that he grabbed the rope that let the hot air out of the balloon. There was a hiss and we dropped sharply back into the cloud. "More straw and wool on the burner, Nell!" Pa told me.

"We've none left," I told him. "We just had enough to get across the river but we've already used too much getting free of the prison wall," I told him. "Looks like we'll land in the river and drown after all," I said.

I looked over the side to see if Theus was still with us. He'd be all right. He could swim and maybe drown, but he could come back to life; swim and drown and come back to life as many times as he liked until he reached safety. I couldn't.

"Are you still there, Theus? Those birds have lost us a lot of smoke. We're going down."

"They weren't birds," he called up. "That was the Avenger – the one that's hunting me. It has the help of Achilles and Paris and it looked like a Hecatonchires too."[30]

---

30 I know what you think: if Theus saw them then why didn't they see him? Well, if you are in a mist then it hides you from someone outside the mist. But often you can look out and see people outside. Oh, I know what I mean. Anyway, Theus came out of the cloud when they had passed and he saw their backs quite clearly.

We dropped through the underside of the cloud. Theus waved his free hand and I looked for the oily waters of the river, waiting to suck us under to a clammy death. Instead I saw bright fires in the centres of circles of tents and I knew Pa had had a second "forgetting". "Pa!" I cried. "Did you remember to check the wind? Was it blowing from the east or the west before we left Eden City?"

He shrugged. "They said it blows from the west in the evenings."

"Well they were wrong. We aren't heading to East River City – we're heading over the plains to the camps of the Wild Folk!"

"That's never happened to me in all my years as a balloonist," he said.

"All your years? Yesterday was the first time you've ever flown free…"

"The Montgolfier Brothers in Paris…"

"No, Pa!" I yelled at him. "That was just a story you made up to fool the suckers, remember? You're not really a balloonist… you're a showman."

"I guess you're right, Nell," he said sadly.

"And you're soon going to be a scalped showman," I moaned.

We dropped steadily towards a circle of tents and warriors suits made of animal skins came out to watch us. They mostly carried stone-headed hatchets and bows and arrows. I guessed it would be the hatchets they used to scalp us.

It would hurt. I hoped the landing would kill us first.

But the landing was gentle as a feather on a sheet of silk. I was forgetting that Theus was a flier. He landed first. He placed the cannon on the soft grass – prairie grass that had been cropped short by the Wild Folk's ponies – then he reached up and held the basket in his powerful arms.

He lowered us onto the grass. Pa snatched his hat and jammed it on his head.

"That won't stop them scalping you," I said.

"It's not meant to!" he replied. "If we are going to go then let's give them a show!"

"What?"

"Let's do what we did when we landed in Eden City and put on a show for the Wild People. They've probably not seen anything like us before. These simple folk may even think we're gods come down from the sky!"

"Uh?"

Pa was usually right. I hurried to dress as Miss Cobweb and looked for somewhere to string a tightrope. The Wild Folk's tents were pointed at the top – a rope could go from tent-top to tent-top, I thought.

I whispered a quick order to Theus because he was tall enough to reach the tent-tops without ladders. He took the rope from the cannon and set to work. Pa worked out what we were doing and started his show.

"Welcome to Doctor Dee's most amazing Carnival of Danger!" he said and smiled at the puzzled warriors. "This evening you will see my talented team of plucky performers daring to defy death. In fact, my friends, I have to warn you some of them may *not* survive the dangers. Some days Death wins. If you are upset by the sight of mangled bodies and bleeding corpses then please go home now…"

No one moved. No one smiled. He turned to the basket and coughed. "*Miss Cobweb…*" he said loudly and paused. He looked towards the basket with a frown. "… will not just walk on the wire, she will *dance* on the wire!" He dropped his voice. "Are you ready yet, Nell?"

"I can't find the frilly pants for Miss Cobweb!" I squeaked back.

"Go on without them!"

"What!" I squawked. "Dance on the rope with no pants? No thanks!"

"Would you rather lose your scalp?"

"Well, Pa, yes I *would* if I have to choose!" I dived back in the basket and rooted in the clothes box.

Pa turned back to the ring of warriors. "While we wait I will show you my fabulous fire-eating act!" he told them. He took a small bottle of spirits from his coat pocket and sipped some. Then he marched to the log fire and pulled a long stick from it. He blew out a great globe of flame like a ball of fire.

Audiences normally screamed at this and children hid behind their mother's skirts. The Wild Folk stayed silent. I found the pants and pulled them on.

Pa tried every fire trick he knew but the Wild Folk kept their faces as stony as their axe-heads. Pa finished by spitting three fire-balls into the air – one after the other and lit the night sky. It was a sensation. He swept off his top hat and took a bow.

The warriors shook their heads and looked at a boy about my age. He wore trousers made of animal skin but no shirt. He stepped forwards and took the flaming stick from Pa.

The boy placed the burning end against his bare arm and ran it up and down, then he ran it over his chest. My mouth fell open with horror but the boy showed no pain and no burns. He turned and used the stick to scatter some of the fire's glowing ashes over the earth. Then he stepped into the ashes and walked slowly across them.

The boy stepped in front of Pa and took a bow. The warriors cheered and laughed. Pa clapped politely with a wide but worried grin.

"Now, famous Miss Cobweb from England – in her famous frilled pants – will dance on the rope! Give her a warm round of applause!" he clapped wildly. No one joined in.

Theus lifted me onto the rope. I had to walk and dance with no net below me. It was high enough to break a few bones and some of my wobbles were real. I finished with a spin, a bow and jumped into Theus's waiting arms.

The Wild Folk boy ran up the sloping side of the tent with no help. He jumped onto the rope and he didn't walk it or dance it. He did tumbles and cartwheels across it. He swung from it, balanced on it and leaped across it. He dropped off it, caught it with one arm and let himself drop to the ground. This time he walked over to me and bowed as his friends cheered.

I felt my face going redder than our balloon's red stripes. He'd made me look the biggest fool ever to step off a balloon. That's when Theus, the hero, stepped forwards and saved my blushes.

He walked up to the smirking boy and took the hatchet from his belt. Then he placed his hand on a rock and brought the sharp edge down suddenly. Theus's finger flew off and into the fire.

The boy looked stunned. I thought Pa was going to faint. I was the only one who knew Theus would grow a new liver before the day had passed – I guessed he could grow a new finger.

Theus passed the hatchet back to the boy and tilted his head as if to say, "Your turn."

The boy shook his head slowly. "You win," he said. Then he turned to me and Pa and said, "I knew you Wild People were crazy but I didn't know you were *that* crazy."

"You speak English?" I asked.

He shrugged. "We tried to trade with the Wild People behind the wooden walls. We learned."

"We're not Wild People," I said.

"You come from the place they call Eden City, don't you?"

"Yes."

"We call you the Wild People," he said.

"They call you the Wild Folk!" I told him.

He nodded. "They would."

"You're not Wild? You don't scalp people?" I asked.

He gave a small smile. "Never. It's a story they put about to make the Wild People... I mean the people of Eden City... to make them fear us and kill us when they have the chance."

"We're not really from Eden City," Pa told the boy. "We're travellers. We belong nowhere."

The boy's smile was wide and bright now. "So are we. My people roam the plains hunting and fishing. We have no towns like Eden City."

"*Your* people?" Theus asked. "You are a chief?"

The boy nodded. "I am called Running Bear."

"Because you run around with no clothes on?" I asked.

The boy threw up his eyes. "Bear... the big furry

animal. I don't run around *bare* naked."

"Sorry," I muttered.

"My father was the bravest of the brave," he said. "But the Wild People of Eden City have special weapons they call guns. They use fire and spit out metal bullets. They killed him. Even my father couldn't face the Eden City bullets and live."

"Sorry," Theus said.

"Sorry?"

"For giving them fire. I stole it and gave it to humans. I had no idea..." he began. He looked at his feet, suddenly ashamed. "They will use their metal guns to destroy us in time," the boy said.

"Is that why you're attacking Eden City now?" Pa asked. "Trying to kill them before they kill you?"

Running Bear frowned. "No. If we kill all Eden City Wild People they will only send more from over the river. We don't want to kill any of them."

I was puzzled. "You are surrounding the city. They can't get food in and they can't get out. It's a siege."

"Like Troy," Theus put in.

Running Bear spread his hands. "The mayor said his name was Making Peace..."

"Mayor Makepeace?"

"He told us the people of his city wanted to take our plains and turn them into farms. He said he would give us guns and gold and we could move across the mountains."

"And you don't want to go. That's why you are attacking?" Pa asked.

"No, that is not why. The Mayor of Making Peace said he wanted to talk peace in our camp. He came with his lawmakers and his guns. We talked just a short while. He could see we were never going to give up our lands and he smiled and said he would make us an even richer offer the next day."

"More gold?" Pa asked. Pa liked gold.

"What use is gold to us? No, while the mayor talked of peace his lawman with the hair on his face waited outside..."

"Sheriff Spade?" I nodded.

"Yes. His sheriff. That man stole my baby sister, Prairie Rose, from her tent and carried her back to Eden City. That night he made us his offer... give up our lands and we can have our princess back."

Theus closed his eyes and murmured, "They are holding a princess prisoner in Eden City just as the Trojans held Helen of Sparta."

"My father led a party to rescue her but we cannot climb their walls while they have guns and we have bows," he said and there was pain in his eyes. "They killed him."

"So you have to starve them till they surrender?" I asked.

"Or give up the land. That is our only choice."

There was silence apart from a soft wind blowing the camp fire into crackling sparks.

"It's not your only choice," Theus said.

We all looked at him. "What else can we do?"[31] I asked.

"We can rescue her," Theus said simple. "Rescue their princess from her Troy."

31 I remember saying "we". I don't remember when I decided we were suddenly on the side of the Wild Folk of the plains. But Pa and Theus didn't argue. They must have decided around the same time that we were fighting against Eden City.

FIFTEEN

TROY – 4000 YEARS AGO, AND EDEN CITY – 1795

Those old Greek gods were snobs. They hated the pathetic little humans. But they couldn't stop meddling in human lives. Even when the siege of Troy was over they still wanted more fun. Maybe another siege to play games with ...

Hera and Zeus looked down on Troy from their cloud. It was a sad sight.

The palaces and towers were smoking ruins with black and burnt timber sticking out from charred walls like ribs from a dead dog that birds have torn apart.

Crimson wine flowed down the streets from the fountain and mingled with the cherry red blood of the men and boys.

Everyone seemed to be moving so slowly. The

Trojan women slaves were roped together and driven out over the plains to the waiting boats. Greek soldiers dug wearily on the plains to make deep pits and throw in their victims. They dragged them by the legs and let them slide down into the dusty graves.

Other soldiers sweated with huge tree trunks to lever the stones of the old walls and send them tumbling to ruin. From time to time a voice was raised in anger.

"Oi! Watch where you're tumbling that wall... you nearly hit me with that topless tower."

"You should watch where you're standing, mate!"

"I was *told* to dig this grave here. It's more than my job's worth to move. So be more careful or I'll come in there and shove this spade in your big mouth."

"I'd like to see you try!"

"Oh yeah? You want a fight, do you?"

There was a silence as a thousand soldiers listened and waited. Then, "No... I've been fighting for ten years. Enough's enough. Sorry, mate."

"All right, mate."

And the shovelling, slave-shifting and tumbling went on for a few more days. The Greeks left and the rats returned. The windy plains drifted their sands over the ruins and turned Troy into a memory.

"I'm bored now," Hera said.

Zeus looked at her. "You were *bored* because the siege went on and on. I did something about it. Now you're bored again because the siege is over. You are *never* satisfied, are you?"

The goddess shrugged. "Couldn't you find us another, more exciting siege. One that lasts ten weeks, not ten years?"

Zeus sighed. "As it happens, cousin Theus is at one right now. Mind you it's four thousand years in the future."

"Take me there," Hera ordered. "Does it have a hostage princess? And heroes? And villains? Take me there."

"Oh, all right," Zeus sighed and used his godly powers to move the cloud from the windy plains of Troy to the windy plains of Eden City.[32]

---

32 The ordinary gods had to fly through space to move through time, of course. But Zeus was no ordinary god. He was chief god and he could move through time and space with a special power that no one else had. It was a power he rarely used – so he's not likely to pop up and look over your shoulder as you read this. The truth is he was too lazy to enjoy this wonderful gift. He had to be nagged by someone like Hera. I am nagged by my landlord to pay the rent, so I write this book. We all need a little push from time to time, don't we?

As the cloud moved round to the other side of the Earth, the Sun (that makes time) began to spin through the sky faster and faster till it was a blur.

There are 365 days in a year and the Earth spun through nearly 4,000 years. Four thousand times 365. That's… a lot.

The spinning slowed and Zeus's cloud arrived above the plains of Eden City. Zeus and Hera studied the people. "This time *I* want to join in. I can't spend my life sitting here just watching the little human theatre. I want to be on the stage, acting. Tell me what to do."

Zeus was pleased to let Hera take over. It would give him a rest… I *told* you he was lazy. So he explained to her about disguising herself and he told her about the plot to break the city defences. Then she lowered herself to Earth and arrived in the middle of Running Bear's camp at sunrise. It was the morning after we'd arrived in the middle of the night. Everyone was sleepy. That's when I first saw her. We were heating some corn meal into a porridge for breakfast when she walked into the circle of tents.

She looked like a warrior queen in bronze armour and carrying a shield and spear. The Wild Folk looked at her as if she were a being from another planet. "Greetings, simple human creatures," she said.

Running Bear jumped to his feet and faced her. Hera had got her size a little wrong and she was too tall for a human woman. Running Bear and I came up to the buckle of her belt. "We are not simple," the boy told her.

"And we're not creatures," I added.

She ignored us. "I am come among you to rescue your princess from the evil city!" she said as if she was an actress on the stage or Pa trying to attract a crowd.

"We already have a plan," I told her.

It was almost as if she was deaf.

"I have made a fine wooden statue of a horse!" she said and pointed through a gap between the tents to where a carved horse stood on wheels. It was as high as the walls of Eden City and very life-like. "Your soldiers can enter the city inside the horse and massacre their men and boys as they sleep."

"We don't want to massacre anyone," Theus said. "We have a plan just to rescue the princess…"

She looked at him. "Oh, it's you Theus. Trust you to try to protect your precious little humans. You can't make a sacrifice without killing goats, we always say.

You can't rescue a princess without a good old massacre. Look at Troy."

"I have a plan…" Theus began.

"A plan? Hah! The simple plans are always the best. I will go into the city, inside the horse, and open the gates at night. You bring your army in to kill the men and boys. Simple."

"There's no need for anyone to die," Theus started to argue but Hera had closed her ears again.

"Blood will flow in the streets!" the goddess cried. "The princess will be returned to her happy husband…"

"She doesn't have a husband… she's not a year old," Running Bear tried to explain.

"The city shall be burned to the ground!" she cried. Then she looked around the warriors who were spooning porridge into their mouths from their wooden bowls. "Who will join me inside the horse and bring glory to the tribe?"

The warriors looked at one another. One spoke up. "Has it got a toilet inside?" he asked.

"Of course not!" Hera told him.

"Then you won't get me up in that!" he said and the others nodded.

"Then I shall go alone. All the great heroes of the world must fight alone. The glory shall be mine, all mine!" she cried. "I'll just get inside and you can pull it to the gates of the city," she added.

We rose wearily. "Where did *she* come from?" I muttered to Theus.

He sighed. "Sorry," he told me. "That's my cousin Hera in disguise. The wife of cousin Zeus."

He looked up at a lonely cloud in the morning sky over the camp. He saw something I couldn't see. He waved, then smiled. "Yes, Zeus is here."

I squinted at the bright cloud but saw nothing but a golden glow that could have been the morning sun reflected. "What do we do?"

"Let her try," I suppose. "We have nothing to lose. The main thing is that the baby Prairie Rose is rescued."

"What if she kills everyone in Eden City?" I said.

"They have Achilles and Paris to defend them," Theus said. "But she may get through the gates and we can slip in behind her."

As the wooden horse was dragged over the plains Theus told Running Bear of our plan. "Nell and I will go into the city when they open the gates and bring out the princess."

"I'll come with you," the boy said.

"No," Theus told him. "You look like one of the Wild Folk. They will kill you as soon as they see you inside the city."

Running Bear grumbled and argued but had to give way in the end. We walked behind the wooden horse and it came to rest about fifty paces from the gates of Eden City. Theus and I lay in the long grass and waited.

As the morning passed the Wild Folk's tents were taken down and the warriors moved back to the foothills of the mountains, out of sight. The people of Eden City came to the walls to look at the strange horse.

In the afternoon the gates swung open and we heard footsteps in the long grass. "Well, well, well! A wooden horse!" Mayor Makepeace said.

The voice of the sheriff laughed. "That old trick from the story of Troy, eh?"

Theus moved sharply and whispered, "Even after all this time you humans remember the story of Troy?"

"Of course! I would have told your Hera that but she didn't seem to be listening," I told him.

"So the horse trick won't work a second time?"

"Not even Mayor Makepeace is *that* stupid," I said.

Sure enough the mayor said, "Grab some dried grass and pile it up under the horse. If it's wood it'll burn."

There was a rustling as the sheriff and his helpers gathered grass. Then there was a crackling when they set fire to it.

"Should we go and look at that balloon out there on the plain? See if that robbing, cheating, lying Doctor Dee's around?" the mayor asked.

"No, the Wild Folk will have him by now. He'll be scalped and most likely eaten," I heard the sheriff say.

"Lucky man."

"Lucky?"

"Yep. Lucky. Because scalped and eaten is *nothing* to what the people of Eden City would have done if they'd got their hands on him."

"True," the sheriff chuckled. "Now stand back, mayor. The wooden horse is well alight. Let the Wild Folk inside roast. We'd better get back to the city and watch in comfort."

Even in the shelter of the grass we could hear the roar of the fire.

We looked up and saw the flames wrap themselves

around the body of the horse. There was a hideous scream. "This isn't how it's supposed to go!" Hera cried. "I'm burning!"

The heat and the smoke drifted over to our hiding place. We raised our heads just enough to see the party from Eden City walk back through the walls laughing. The gates slammed behind them.

The horse burned fiercely then the legs began to crumble to ashes and the body crumpled to the ground before it fell apart in a shower of sparks.

Hera stood in the glowing ashes of the wooden horse. Her shining armour was soot, her hair was black dust under her helmet and her shield a smouldering, twisted ruin. "Zeus!" she cried to the sky. "I want to go home! Take me away from these *dreadful* people at once! If that simple tribe want their princess back then Theus can just get on with it."

I heard the gasps from the watchers on the Eden City walls as Hera rose up towards the cloud and the cloud sped over the mountains and disappeared.

The wind on the plains blew the ashes into a swirling cloud and the grass swished and swayed. Then Theus gripped my arm and held it tight. He pointed towards the city and then used that finger to press against his lips. His godly ears could hear something. As they came closer I could hear the footsteps for myself. They stopped and a creaking voice spoke. A voice so cruel it chilled me to my toes and froze me up to my hair.

"So, Achilles, our friend Theus has a plan to enter the city and rescue this princess, has he?"

"Yes, Avenger, that's what it sounded like to me," a young man replied.

"Then we'll be waiting for him," the evil voice cackled.

"We don't know *how* he'll try to get into Eden City, Avenger. It's guarded better than Troy. You Greeks took ten years to get in there," another young man put in.

"But we got you in the end, Paris," the first young man said.

"Only with that stupid horse trick..."

"Stop arguing," the Avenger hissed. "The Greeks didn't have one of those balloon things. Theus has. Look. Now the tents have gone you can see it lying out on the plain."

"So?" Achilles asked.

"So, when it gets dark Theus will fly the balloon

over the walls of the city and rescue the princess," the Avenger said.

"How do you know?" Paris asked.

"Because that's what I'd do if I were Theus. But he doesn't know, I'll be waiting for him and I will destroy him forever!"

"No, no!" Paris argued. "The Greeks got away with it because they *hid* their raiders inside the horse. Theus can't hide the balloon. As soon as the Eden City guards see the balloon they'll shoot at him with their guns."

The Avenger seemed to stamp its foot. "Then Theus needs some help. He needs something to get the guards off the walls. Something to make them keep their heads down while he flies over."

"Something like the Hecatonchires?" Paris asked.

"Exactly," the Avenger hissed. "We send our friend Hec to help Theus. But we know he'll be helping Theus to land in my waiting claws!"

"Sounds a good plan," Achilles agreed.

"So go and get Hec from his hiding place in the ship. Fly him over to the plains and tell him to wait beside the balloon. Tell him to help Theus."

"Do you think Theus will use Hec to help? It's a risk." Paris asked.

"I know Theus and I know his weakness – he will take risks... and he's stupid enough to fall for it. No one escapes the Avenger for long. Prometheus must be destroyed. Tonight is his last night on Earth. Ever!"

SIXTEEN

EDEN CITY – 1795, EVENING

Sometimes it's hard to be a writer. So many things were happening in Eden City and around it that it's hard to remember which order they happened in. Try to follow...

When the Wooden Horse of Eden City went up in flames the Wild Folk warriors came back from the hills and set up their camps on the plains again.

Theus and I sat gloomily by the balloon while Pa worked to patch it up. "If the Avenger is waiting for me I'll never get to the Temple of the Hero inside the city. I'll never find out who that human hero was and win my freedom."

"And Pa and I will never be able to fly back to East River City and spend the loot he stole from

Eden City," I said.

"And Running Bear will never get his sister free."[33]

As the sun fell in an orange ball below the mountains Running Bear called a council of war.

All we seemed to talk about was what we COULDN'T do.

… we *can't* climb the walls because the defenders have guns and they'd shoot us all…

… we *can't* fly over the walls in the balloon – even if the wind changes the guards would shoot us down…

… we *can't* fire Theus over the walls in the cannon – he'd be killed and could come back to life, but the Avenger will find him and destroy him before Prairie Rose is rescued…

… we *can't* march up to the gates and ask to get in because the people of Eden City are after Pa and want their money back…

… we *can't* send Theus or Pa or Running Bear into the city at all…

---

33 Everyone likes a good moan at times. But that evening we had more moans than a porcupine has quills. If moans were bones we'd have filled a graveyard. We were down, defeated and desperate. Next time YOU feel like a moan just remember how miserable WE were. You could NEVER get as moanful as we were.

… we *can't* send me in because, even if I rescued the Wild Folk's princess I couldn't get her out.

Theus said, "The Hecatonchires will be here soon… don't be afraid. It looks like a monster but with one brain shared between fifty heads it isn't very clever." He told us what Hec would look like and how it had been useful at Troy – scaring the guards away from the walls.

And that's when I had my idea. An idea that COULD work.

The Hecatonchires landed with a clatter of wings in the centre of the tent circle. If the warriors were afraid then they didn't show it. Theus had told me what to expect but it was still a weird sight. "Hello, lads!" 10 of the heads said.

"Hello, Hec," Theus said and stepped forwards. "It's good to see you!"

"Is it?" head 35 said. Head 7 added, "That's odd. We spent all our life in the Underworld. Humans were sent down there and when they saw us they screamed!" Head 37 agreed. "That's right. No one's *ever* said it's good to see me!"

"Well, we are, aren't we?" Theus said and swung

round the circle to include us all.

"Yes!" we all cried.

"But why?" Hec head 35 asked.

"Because you are a legend. We've heard what you did at Troy – battered the walls till the guards fled," Theus said. "We were just saying, we could do with a Hecatonchires if we're going to attack Eden City, weren't we?"

Again we all nodded and agreed.

"That's strange," head 25 put in, "because we've come here tonight to help you to do exactly the same!"

"We know…" I began until Pa slapped a hand round my big mouth and hissed, "No, we're not *supposed* to know that!"

"Mng-Mng!" I said (which, as you know, was meant to be 'sor-ry!').

"The moon rises at midnight," Theus said. "We will go into action then." He looked at me. "I don't like the plan. But I don't see any other way."

Pa added, "If *you're* worried about the plan then how do you think *I* feel?"

Sheriff Spade sat in *The Storm Inn* and pulled at his

moustaches nervously.[34] The mayor patted his arm, filled his ale pot and leaned towards him. "Don't worry," he said. "If a wooden horse is the best they can come up with then we have nothing to fear from the Wild Folk."

"The people of Eden City are getting hungry," the sheriff said. "Another week and they'll be getting angry. They'll turn against us. They'll make us hand the Wild Folk's princess back and stop this siege."

The mayor's little eyes glittered in the candlelight. "If that happens then we must force the Wild Folk to go away."

"We haven't enough bullets and powder," Sheriff Spade groaned. "We could have gone out and killed them all if that Doctor Dee had kept his promise and brought us fresh powder and guns."

"We'll deal with him some other time. We may not have enough powder to attack but we have enough to defend."

"But if we *don't* attack we'll just stay here till we

34 No, I wasn't there myself but the bar manager was. Later, when I went back to Eden City, I heard his story and put it together. It almost happened the way I tell it – and *almost* is as good as some stories get.

starve and the Eden City people rebel, Mayor Makepeace. We've *lost* thanks to that showman with the balloon."

"We don't need bullets while we have the princess. I have a second plan. We simply put her in a cradle and hang the cradle over the side of the Eden City walls. The Running Bear brat will hear his little sister crying as she gets hungry."

"He won't give in."

"Then he'll hear her *stop* crying after a while. *That* is the worst sound of all. The silence will be like poison in his ear. He'll think she's dying. He *will* give in. And then…"

"And then we take over the plains from here to the mountains," the sheriff said and supped his ale and smacked his lips.

"You and me, Spade. We will own it," the mayor breathed. "Thousands of acres of rich land. And we will sell it to settlers and farmers for five dollars an acre. Riches beyond your dreams, Spade. Beyond your dreams." The mayor's greed gripped his throat and made his voice hoarse. "That baby will make us rich, rich, *rich, rich, RICH!*"

The sheriff stopped with his ale pot halfway to his

mouth. "So shouldn't we be guarding the baby if she's that precious?"

"Waters will take care of it. You'll see. Everything will work out fine."

Achilles sat on the floor of the Temple of the Hero and sharpened the blade of his spear. Paris sat beside him and worked on his arrow heads.

"Why are we here?" Paris asked.

"Because the Avenger told us it's a good place to wait," Achilles said for the fifth time. "The Avenger is in the sky over the city waiting for the balloon to arrive. As soon as it starts to come down he'll call us and we'll fight off Theus's friends while the Avenger grabs Theus."

"But why are we *here*?" Paris asked.

"I've just told you!" Achilles exploded and shook the cobwebs from the walls.

"I know. I know you said that. But *why* is it a good place to wait? Why are we in a temple and who is the hero?" Paris went on.

Achilles rose and stretched. "No one ever comes here, it seems. And the hero? His statue is over there by the altar."

"It's covered up. I can't see his face," Paris complained.

"That's to keep the dust off."

"Can we have a look?" Paris asked.

"A look?"

"At the statue. See what this Eden City hero looks like?"

"It will probably look like me," Achilles said and walked over the dusty floor to the altar.

It was lit by a candle. The only light in the cold and gloomy temple. Achilles lifted the corner of the cloth and looked under it. "Well, well, well... would you believe it?"

"That's odd," Paris said with a frown.

"Very odd," Achilles agreed and lowered the cloth again.

The Avenger hung on its huge wings, high over the plains. It was sure Prometheus, the Fire Thief, was down there somewhere. But he would be lost in the swarms of Wild Folk. It was best to stick to the plan and wait for the god to enter the city and try to rescue the baby.

The Avenger knew they would use the balloon.

They would light the fire beneath the basket and lift into the air. The Fire Thief would be lifted by the power of the fire Prometheus gave to the humans. It was fire that would carry Prometheus into the city. It was fire that would carry Prometheus to his destruction. The Avenger liked that idea. "Serves him right," it cawed as it soared.

But the balloon lay where it had landed. The fire-box was cold and still. It was near midnight now and no one moved to touch the empty bag of the balloon.

The grass of the plains rippled in the thin moonlight and the Avenger's eagle eyes saw people moving towards the city. A Wild Folk boy, a girl and a tall man in a top hat.

If they were planning a rescue then Theus was not with them. The Avenger swooped down low and saw the boy was carrying a fine rope and the girl held a leather bag while the man dragged a wooden tube on wheels behind him.

A little further behind the Avenger spotted the Hecatonchires as it lumbered along behind them. It wondered who they were and it kept watching. The Avenger understood. This little army would attack the walls and drive the defenders back. But

Prometheus would not climb the walls here. "Of course he won't!" the Avenger hissed. "The city will rush to defend the west wall. Prometheus will climb the wall somewhere else. Maybe he'd even come in from the east – the river!"

That was a clever plan, the Avenger decided. It worked it out. The Wild Folk had lots of canoes on the river. While the defenders hurried to the west wall Prometheus would slip quietly onto the quayside, steal the baby and escape.

"I'm a fool!" the big bird howled. "Getting to the baby will be easy. But it would be tricky to climb back over the walls with a child. It would make much more sense to come by river. I see it all now! And if he does slip past me I have those fools Achilles and Paris waiting to snatch him at the Temple of the Hero. Prometheus will be mine before sunrise."

The Avenger cackled with a noise that sounded like a strangled rooster.[35] It beat its golden-brown wings and climbed high. Then it half closed those wings and sped down towards the quayside. It landed close to

---

35 I know this because, of course, I was on the plain below when the Avenger cackled. I guess the miserable monster didn't do a lot of laughing and that's why its laugh sounded so strained.

The Storm Inn and walked across the road to hide in the dark alley by the side.

A small figure with a dirty handkerchief stepped out and threw an arm around the Avenger's neck. In his hand was a knife with a broken blade. "Your money or your life!" the little robber growled.

"Oh, not you again, Mr Waters. Go away, will you, I'm busy."

"Oops! Sorry, sir. Didn't recognise you," the old man said. "Guess I'll go and rob someone else."

"Yes, you do that."

"Goodnight!"

"Oh, I'll have a *very* good night."

But the Avenger was wrong. The Avenger was double-wrong.

Wrong about Theus coming from the river.

Wrong about having a good night…

SEVENTEEN

EDEN CITY − 1795, MIDNIGHT

How would you do it? Climb into an enemy city, rescue a baby AND get it out of the city? Don't know, do you? Now here's the thing. Neither did I. Oh yes, I'll tell you how I planned to do those things. But Pa, Running Bear and Prometheus were so dazzled by my plan they missed the one thing WRONG with the plan. There would be no escape for ME at the end of it. No plan is perfect − not even mine. But I didn't know that then.

The Hecatonchires lumbered along and stopped about a hundred paces from the wooden walls of Eden City. It began to pick up stones from the windy plains of Eden City. I was hoping to surprise the defenders but with Hec there was no chance.

He just *had* to talk to himself...

"Left... two-three-four-five... and right... two-three-four-five!" the heads chanted. "Left... two-three-four-five... and right... two-three-four-oops! Well, it's a bit dark out here!" After a minute a hundred rocks were clutched in a hundred hands. "Righty-ho! Ready when you are."

There was excited chatter from the guards on the walls of Eden City as they stared into the moonlit gloom. They saw the fifty-headed monster but they didn't quite believe it. They were slow to raise their muskets.

Too slow.

Suddenly a hundred arms threw a hundred rocks at them. Some clattered off the wooden walls – *thunk* – some sailed over into the streets behind them – *clatter* – and some bounced off the heads of the slower soldiers – *ouch*.

It went silent. In the dim light the guards shrank down behind the parapet and heard distant voices... "Left... two-three-four-five... and right... two-three-four-five!"

Guard Hank Plank of River Row muttered, "Got to go home. I just remembered... I need to put the cat out."

"Is it on fire?" his friend Joe Scrimger asked.

Hank shuffled over to the ladder and jumped down two rungs at a time. "I think he's scared," Joe scoffed. "It'll take more than a hundred stones to scare me…"

"Righty-ho! Ready when you are," came the cheerful voice from the plains. There was a thunderous rumble as rocks rained down.

"Ooo! It would take more than a hundred rocks… but two hundred are just ninety-nine too many. No one will miss me if I go home to put my wife out!" Joe Scrimger whined and headed for the ladder. It was tough getting down. Tough when twenty other guards were all trying to climb down the same ladder.

"We don't get paid for this," a voice grumbled in the darkness. "Careful, you're standing on my fingers!"

"No… it's someone else's turn to do guard duty," another voice agreed.

By the time the third storm of stones sailed over the walls they were deserted. The gallant guards of Eden City had torn back through the twisted streets of their city and were hiding under their blankets. Fifty cats had been put out… even though not one of them was on fire.

Only an old man wandered the deepest shadows of

the darkest alleys with a dirty handkerchief around his face, looking for someone to rob.

Outside the walls we sensed the silence of the city. A soft sighing of the wind through the grass was answered by the yowls of fifty sleepy cats. "Time to go," I said.

Theus looked unhappy. "This is a job for me," he said for the twentieth time.

For the twentieth time I told him, "No. You've done your part. You've worked out where they're hiding the baby princess."

"I could be wrong," he argued.

"That's a chance I'll have to take," I said and I closed my eyes and tried to remember the map he had drawn me.

Running Bear fastened the light rope around the end of an arrow and fired it at the wall. It struck the parapet and sank into the wood quite deeply… at least I was hoping it was deep.

He took the loose end of the rope and tied it around the heaviest thing he could find… a leg of the Hecatonchires.

"Step back, Hec," Pa ordered. The monster obeyed. The rope went tight. Pa checked it. "Perfect," he told me. "So long as the creature doesn't move."

"I'm not a creature," Hec complained. "I'm a people just like you."

"Except you have fifty heads," Pa told him.

"Yeah, and fifty times as much hurt feelings!"

"Sorry, sorry, Hec," I said quickly. "I am so-o-o grateful to you. I wish there was some way I could repay you."

"Huh! Huh!" the monster giggled. "You could give us a kiss before you go."

"Oh, all right," I agreed. Hec lifted me up with his lower hands and passed me up, hand over hand, till I reached his shoulders. Then I kissed him... fifty times.

"Cor, I've never been kissed before," he sighed.

"Look, can we just get on with this rescue?" Pa snapped.

"We're ready," Running Bear said.

I stepped onto the rope and began to walk along it, climbing all the time. The wind from the plains rocked me but I knew I would never fall. It was just too important. Even the cats had fallen silent by the time I reached the top of the wall and climbed over onto the parapet. The guards had all gone, I was pleased to see.

I tugged on the rope. I felt it go slack as Hec stepped forwards. Pa untied it from his leg and tied it to the cannon. I hauled the cannon carefully up the wall. Even though it was made of wood it took all my strength. Sweat ran down my face and made the palms of my hands slippery. I didn't want it to tip and spill what was in the barrel.

It was hard to heave it over the wall and I was sweating. Then I lowered it down the other side into the street below. Now there was no way back for me. I had to go on with the plan.

I climbed carefully down the ladder. There was no hurry. I had all night.

I reached in to the barrel of the cannon and pulled out the two bundles inside. I unwrapped the soft one – a bundle of clothes, a hat, boots, a wig and my Gregory the Great moustache.

I dressed carefully. I may not be able to shape-shift like Zeus but I could do a good job of looking like someone else.

The second bundle was a leather bag. I slipped that inside my jacket pocket.

Finally I gathered stones from the street – stones that Hec had thrown – and put them under the barrel of the cannon so it pointed up to the dark sky. I set the cannon so it would fire at a touch of the trigger.

I closed my eyes and tried to picture Theus's map. I knew it would be too dark to read a map in the dingy Eden City streets and I didn't dare to show a light.

It was a slow and stumbling journey. For some reason there were a lot of cats wandering around, green eyes glowing angrily, mewling at doors.

An old man stepped out from one dark alley and waved a broken knife in front of me. "Your money or your life?" he croaked. "I am the Phantom of the Night!"

The rescue plan was that I'd dress and act like Sheriff Spade. I had to put the plan into action a little earlier than I meant to. "Put that knife down or I'll arrest you in the name of the law!" I said in the sheriff's creaky voice.

"Is that you, sheriff?"

"It is."

"Oh, this just hasn't been my night."

A little starlight drifted down into the street and my eyes were used to the dark now. "Say... didn't I buy you a drink in *The Storm Inn* last night?" I asked angrily. I'd felt sorry for this old man and now he was trying to rob me.

"No, sheriff, *I* bought *you* a drink!"

"Ah, yes… oh… ah, so you did, old man. But wasn't there a girl in the bar that bought you a drink? That sweet and pretty girl that was with Doctor Dee's Carnival of Danger?"

"I wouldn't call her pretty, but, yes, she did buy me a drink," the old man admitted.

"So you should be ashamed of yourself!" I told him. "Why?"

"Because someone shows you kindness and that's how you repay them," I raged.

"But she was a sucker. I always take money from suckers, same as you, Sheriff Spade."

"Ah, yes… oh… ah, well it's time you changed your ways."

"And will you be changing *your* ways, sheriff?" he asked me. "I get a few cents from people… but you're planning to rob the Wild People of tens of thousands of dollars worth of land."

"That's different," I told him. "Now take me to Mrs Waters's baby farm," I told him. If anyone could guide me through these dark and twisting streets it would be this old robber.

"I will… I was just on my way there now."

"You were? Why?"

"Because I live there – you know that, sheriff. I'm Josh Waters and my wife runs the baby farm!"

"I knew that," I said quickly. "I was just… checking you are who you say you are."

"Say, are you all right, sheriff?"

"Perfectly. Now lead on," I said and grabbed his greasy belt at the back so I didn't lose him in the dark.

We trotted on through mud and cats till we came to the dusty window and looked into a room lit by a single mutton-fat candle. "Now here's the plan," I told Josh Waters… even though I'd just made up a new plan. "We are going to send the Wild Folk baby back to her people. They'll go away and we'll take over the land. You are going to help me."

"Why am I going to do that, sheriff?" he asked.

I reached inside my jacket and pulled out Pa's money. "For fifty dollars," I said.

"A hundred," he said.

I thought about it. The well-fed baby was princess Prairie Rose. The others were just poor kids that parents didn't want. They were skinny and weak. I changed my plan again. "I'll pay a hundred… *IF* you help me send *ALL* the babies over to the Wild Folk…

they'll care for them better than your wife."

The old man cackled and his breath was more sour than the Eden City gutter we stood in. "Heh! Heh! For a hundred dollars I'll throw in my wife!"

"There are six babies in there that I can see. We can carry three each… you go in and get them."

"Why me?"

"Because I am paying you a hundred dollars and because if your wife wakes up and catches you then you can think up some story."[36]

The old man unlocked the door and a moment later he appeared with three sleepy babies in his arms. "Fifty dollars worth here," he said.

I paid him. He slipped back in and came out with Prairie Rose and another two. I knew it was the princess because she was chubby and better fed than the other children, thin as rain water. She was sleeping happily. "Another fifty," he said.

I paid him again.

The babies were too weak to cry so no one

36 In my first plan I was just going to break open the door. If Mrs Waters had caught me I was going to use the money to buy the princess off her. Old Josh saved me a lot of trouble – even if it cost me half the money Pa had taken from the Eden City people. Well, it wasn't our money anyway.

disturbed us as we hurried back to the walls.

"Hey! I'll use that hundred dollars to buy a new knife," the old man chuckled. "Some feller in a feathered cloak smashed my old one," he told me.

"Feathered cloak?"

"Yep! And a mouth like a beak."

"The Avenger," I said and shivered. I remembered what Theus had told me about it. "Where is it now?"

"I left it on the kitchen table."

"The Avenger's on your kitchen table?"

"No, the broken knife!"

"I mean where is the feller with the feathered cloak?"

"Hiding in an alley at the side of *The Storm Inn*," he told me.

That bit of news was going to be worth the hundred dollars I paid him.

"Where are we going?" the old man asked.

"Wait and see," I said as I reached the spot where I'd hidden the cannon. I took off my black coat and laid my three babies on it while I ran up the steps to the top of the wall. I looked out over the windy plain and saw Big Hec sitting on the ground plucking stalks of grass to chew in each of his mouths. "Hec!" I hissed.

"There'll be *six* of them!"

"Not a problem for me, Nell... I can manage a hundred!"

"Don't drop any," I warned and ran back down.

I took Prairie Rose from Old Josh and slipped her into the barrel of the cannon. I checked it carefully, took aim and fired. The bundle wrapped in the dirty grey blanket shot up into the dead air of Eden City, over the walls and into the clean, free air of the plains.

Then I followed with the other five sleeping children.

I raced up the steps to the top of the walls and looked out. Hec waved his 94 free arms. "They're safe," he cried and turned to walk back to the Wild Folk's camp.

I pulled up the rope I'd used to lower the cannon. I threw it out onto the plains.

"Hey! Who's going to hold the rope?"

The rope hung down the wall. I guessed I would have to climb down that rope rather than tightrope walk it.

But I couldn't climb down the rope. Because someone was climbing up it...

EIGHTEEN

EDEN CITY – *THE STORM INN*, THE WEST WALL, THE TEMPLE OF THE HERO (AND OTHER PLACES)

There were so many things about to happen it's hard to get them in the right order so you understand. It is tough being a writer. Maybe I should try something simpler – like climbing mountains blindfolded.

The Avenger waited in the alley by the side of *The Storm Inn*. Even in the darkness it could see that the Wild Folk's canoes were being paddled *away* from the city. "They'll land and launch another attack on another part of the walls. A single canoe will slip in for the rescue. Oh, it's a cunning plan. There'll be no one left to guard the waterfront."

The Avenger didn't notice that there was already

no one guarding the waterfront.

Inside *The Storm Inn* the mayor and Sheriff Spade supped their ale and chatted about how they would spend their fortunes. "I'll build myself a house in the foothills, away from this stinking city. I may buy myself one of those balloons to fly around the mountains!" the sheriff said.

"The Wild Folk will be in the mountains," the mayor reminded him.

The sheriff frowned. "Talking of Wild Folk, we should be guarding the waterfront in case they decide to land and rescue the baby."

"Another drink and then we'll go," the mayor said.

The landlord had gone to bed hours ago and left the two men with a barrel of ale to serve themselves. As guards go they were as much use to Eden City as a comb to a bald man.

I stood at the top of the west wall of Eden City and shivered. Who was climbing the rope? I stepped back and was ready to make a run for it.

A man's head appeared. He had long hair and a handsome face. "Theus!" I squawked. "You're not supposed to be here. The Avenger's in the city.

We agreed I'd do the rescue alone."

He placed an arm around my shoulder and hugged me. "I know and you did it brilliantly."

In the starlight darkness he couldn't see me blush but I felt my face burning. "So why are you here?"

"I came to look in the Temple of the Hero. I have to find a true human hero so Zeus can set me free. Then I have to go to *The Storm Inn* to get my wings and fly home."

"You can't go to *The Storm Inn*," I said and I told him what old Mr Waters had said.

"Then I'm trapped in Eden City," he said softly.

"No," I said. "*You* go to the temple – I'll get your wings from *The Storm Inn* and bring them to you!"

Theus looked at me curiously. "I think I've found a human hero in you," he said softly.

Now my face turned so red I was surprised it didn't light the city streets like a red moon. I turned to walk down the steps into the city.

"No, Theus, I'm just having fun. This beats tightrope walking for excitement," I laughed. "I'm no hero."[37]

___

37 Go on and argue if you like. Call me a hero – or heroine – if you want. I am far too modest to ever admit it. I only did what any brave, unselfish, wonderful and beautiful girl would do.

He hugged me again. "I'll see you at the Temple of the Hero at sunrise," he said. There was a faint line of charcoal grey on the black horizon over the river. I guessed sunrise wasn't all that far away.

"Let me go first," I said. "We don't want the old man to see you."

He nodded and stayed in the shadow of the wall. I found Mr Waters sitting on the cannon. "Take me to *The Storm Inn*," I told him. "I need to collect something. Then I need you to guide me to the Temple of the Hero."

"*Guide* you, sheriff? You've lived in Eden City all your life.[38] Why would you want me to guide you?"

"For twenty dollars," I said.

"Fifty."

"Ten's my final offer," I said.

"It's a deal," he cackled and I handed over a single dollar. In the darkness he couldn't tell the difference. It was nice to make a sucker of him for a change.

He hobbled through the streets and I held his belt.

---

38   Yes, I'd forgotten I was playing the part of the sheriff. I played so many roles in the carnival I often forgot who I was supposed to be. I had to look at my costume to remind myself. I'll never forget the day Miss Cobweb dived into the flaming pool instead of Captain Dare.

Only the guards who had run away were not asleep. They were waiting for the Wild Folk to rampage down the streets, break into their homes and scalp them in their beds.

Some guards hid under the covers, some hid under the beds and some just crossed their fingers. When morning came, and they discovered the Wild Folk had gone away, they swore that their finger-crossing had worked.

We arrived at *The Storm Inn* in a half-light. I sensed the feathered evil in the alley and crept past.

"Stay here, Mr Waters. I may need you to guide me to the Temple of the Hero." He opened his mouth to speak but I put in, "And, yes, I'll pay you."

I reached for the handle of the tavern door and it turned in my hand.

I jumped back as if it had been a living snake. But it was only the mayor, turning it on the inside as he stepped out. He looked at me and blinked. He looked over his shoulder at the sheriff who stood behind him. "I think I had too much ale," the mayor murmured as he rubbed his eyes. "I'm seeing two sheriffs!"

"No you're not," I said. "That man is a fake and a phoney! He's here to steal the Wild Folk's princess.

I arrest him in the name of the law!"

The sheriff staggered out into the roadway, pushed past the mayor and peered at me. "It's a mirror!"

I had to act quickly or the arrested one would be me and Theus would be trapped. "In fact I don't arrest you... I... er... send you back to the Wild Folk in their boats."

"You what?"

"Mayor! Mr Waters! Grab that phoney sheriff and... and throw him in the river!" I ordered. "Let him swim to the Wild Folk canoes where he came from."

The two men hurried to obey me. That's what fear and panic do to people. All they needed was someone to give them an order and they were happy to obey.

Sheriff Spade struggled and spluttered. The men slithered over the greasy cobbles to the river. When they reached the edge the sheriff found a new strength to struggle. "I'm too old to die!" he cried and grabbed at the mayor as he toppled in. The two fell in the filthy water together and clung to some ropes that hung from a ship. "It's cold!" the mayor wailed.

I hadn't time to listen to them. I ran into the inn and lifted a trapdoor in the stage. The wings were there just as Theus had told me. They were lighter than a spider's web. I tucked them under my arm and ran outside. The sky was pearl grey now and I felt as if a thousand candles were showing the Avenger what I was up to.

The Phantom of the Night had shuffled across the quayside to help the men in the water. "Hurry, Mr. Waters!" I called to the old man who was helping the mayor up to the quayside. "Get back here!"

"In a minute, sheriff," he said as he heaved and struggled with the heavy, soaked man in each hand. He was made heavier by the wet sheriff clinging to his coat tails.

"We don't have a minute," I moaned. With my free hand I pulled out all the cash that was left. "Look, this is all yours if you get me to the Temple of the Hero before sunrise."

Mr Waters grinned his toothless grin. He let the mayor go and I saw him fall back into the water. Mr Waters hobbled across to me. "Why didn't you say so?"

I followed him and half pushed him through the streets. But I knew I'd made a mistake — a mistake as big as Pa had made when he forgot to check the wind. Of course you've spotted it because you are so clever ...

Inside the Temple of the Hero Paris turned his head sharply. "Someone's coming! Footsteps in the courtyard outside," he whispered to Achilles who was resting against the altar. "It's probably Theus."

"Ooh! What do we do?" Achilles said and his voice quivered.

"Hold him till the Avenger gets here. That's what it told us to do."

"We can't hold a god!" Achilles groaned. "You're a human. And I'm only half-god. He'll destroy us. I'm getting out."

Paris jumped to his feet and snatched at Achilles's tunic. "You can't. There's only one door and Theus is coming through it now!"

"Ooh!" Achilles gasped. He jumped onto the altar. A cloth covered the statue. He lifted the cloth and jumped underneath it just as the door creaked open and he heard Theus say, "Paris! What are you doing here?"

"Er... good morning, Theus – just waiting for the Avenger. It told us to wait here for it."

"Us?"

"Ah... yes... Achilles was with me. He's just gone to fetch it."

Theus marched across the dusty temple floor and pushed Paris aside. "Then I'll have to be quick." He lifted the sheet that covered the statue. Carved on the base were the words, '*The hero – he saved us*'.

Then he lifted the cloth higher. The figure underneath was frozen in fear. Theus breathed, "What a wonderful statue. It's almost as if it was alive."

"Yes," Paris laughed nervously.

Theus stepped back and let the cloth fall back in place. "But it's a statue of Achilles. After all my searching Achilles is the hero of Eden City."

"Well, he was a hero at Troy too," Paris said. "Not as good as me, of course. I killed him. But Achilles was a bit of a hero."

"Hang on, Achilles is a half-god. I need to find a *human* hero for Zeus. This is no use to me," Theus moaned. "Now I'll have to fly for my life. I hope Helen gets here in time."

"Helen of Troy?" Paris asked. "The face that launched two hundred ships?"

"No… another, better Helen," Theus said and strode to the door. He looked out into the courtyard. A beautiful young girl was running past an old man.[39] She was carrying his wings under her arm.

Remember, I told you I'd made a mistake? And, of course you spotted it.

I hadn't just told Mr Waters where I was headed with the wings. The Avenger with its eagle ears would have heard me too.

When I reached the mouth of the alleyway that led to the Temple of the Hero I glanced over my shoulder. A shuffling shape of a hunched and feathered figure was following.

I pushed past Mr Waters and raced down the alleyway. Theus was stepping out of the temple followed by Paris.

"Sorry, Theus, the Avenger followed me," I panted. "Hurry or it'll catch you!"

Theus strapped on the wings and looked towards the alley. "Too late," a voice said. The Avenger shuffled past the old man and stopped. Its glittering eyes were deep as a bottomless well. If beaks could grin then its hooked bill was smiling like a cat with a trapped rat.

"Go!" I groaned.

Theus shook his head. "It'll only follow," he sighed.

39   Yes, even under the disguise of a sheriff he could tell she was beautiful. Who was this gallant girl? Oh, come on, who do you think?

"Thanks for trying, Helen of Eden," he said and held me by the shoulders. "But I failed to find the human hero. I'm finished."

I felt a scalding wetness on my cheeks and realized I was crying.

NINETEEN

EDEN CITY – THE TEMPLE OF THE HERO

Well? What did you expect? A happy ending? I'm telling you my true story here. In real life things don't always end happily. So good, kind Theus was caught and doomed. Weep along with me. And then remember... in real life things don't always end happily. Not always. But sometimes they do...

Helen of Eden doesn't give up without a fight.

The Avenger walked slowly forwards to the three steps that led up to the temple where Theus stood.

I snatched Paris's sword from his belt, ran over the courtyard and handed it to the old man. "This feathered feller has a thousand dollars tucked under his wing. Rob him and it's all yours!"

"You want me to do a robbery, sheriff?"

I tore off the moustache and the hat. "I'm not the sheriff."

"Then who did I throw in the river?"

"The real sheriff," I said. "Now quickly, get the money!"

The old man trotted after the Avenger and jumped on its back. He held the sword to its throat – he was careful to keep it out of the way of the crunching beak this time.

The Avenger wasn't expecting it and it toppled over onto its back. "Fly, Theus! Fly!" I cried.

The great god jumped into the air and circled over the temple. "Goodbye, my Helen... you're worth *ten* thousand ships!"

In moments he had disappeared into the clouds. Achilles came out onto the steps and looked at the struggling pair on the ground. Paris looked at him. "Theus thought that *you* were the hero," Paris said. "He never saw the statue of the real hero."

"No," Achilles mumbled, ashamed.

"It was a rotten thing to do to him," Paris said. "We owe him something in return." Achilles nodded. As the Avenger finally threw off the old man the two

Greek warriors threw themselves onto the eagle-bodied monster and wrestled it back down to the ground. The Avenger clawed and slashed with its beak but the two men finally acted like the heroes they were supposed to be.

At last they knelt, one on each of the Avenger's wings and the bird screamed its hatred. "You will go to Hades for this," it cried.

"You were going to take us to Hades anyway, weren't you? Once we helped you capture Theus you'd have betrayed us, wouldn't you?"

"Of course," the Avenger croaked. "Of course."

It lay, helpless, on its back and stared up at the sky. Then its eyes were fixed on something up there. I wondered if Theus had been a fool enough to return. I looked up. A red-and-white striped balloon drifted over the top of the temple and Pa waved down from the basket.

"The wind has changed, Nell!" he shouted. "We're going back to East River City! We'll be free with all that money!"

Then he threw down a rope that I gripped with both hands. I didn't tell him the money was all gone – he may have dropped me! I'd tell him later.

Pa hauled me up into the basket and turned to put more straw on the fire. The balloon leapt into the clouds and carried me away from the filthy city into the clean clouds that glowed gold in the rising sun.

A creature with fifty heads and a hundred arms flew past us on its way to the stars. "Goodbye, Hec!" I called and he waved every arm. Head 35 said, "I'm on my way to a planet I saw on my way here... the people there are normal. They ALL have fifty heads! And the girls are gorgeous!" And he was gone.

Pa looked up at the monster and said, "One day we'll all be able to fly like that," he said. "Go where we want in the air, not be blown by the wind."

"No we won't!" I mocked. "Anyway, it's more fun going where the wind blows you. It's more of an adventure. If humans were meant to fly, the gods would have given us wings."

Pa jammed his top hat firmly on his head as the wind caught the balloon and sent us speeding towards the sunrise side of the river. "One day we'll fly, I tell you. I know it. Trust me. I'm a doctor."

I looked at him and laughed. "No you're not, Pa. No you're not!"

EPILOGUE

EDEN CITY – 1857

That's the end of my story – the story of what happened to me back in 1795. What happened to Helen of Eden City since then? That would take a dozen books to tell. But let me tell you the bits that matter for this story...[40]

Twenty years passed before I returned to Eden City. By then the people had forgotten the showman and the girl who had tricked them out of their money.

I went there on a visit. And now, sixty-two years later, I'm back.

---

40 How Achilles and Paris ended up is in the books of legends. There you'll see they went to the Isles of the Blessed... maybe Zeus felt sorry for them. Or maybe not. For Achilles... yes, Achilles... ended up with his old enemy Helen of Troy. The face that launched a hundred ships. Life is strange. Legend is stranger.

The city has changed. It is dirtier and more twisted than ever with factories spewing purple smoke over the place like a vast umbrella.

The Wild Folk are gone and so are the city's wooden walls. The settlers have moved on to the plains. They used their guns to drive off Running Bear and his people into the mountains where only a few remain now.

Theus would have blamed himself. But, knowing human greed the way I do, I think nothing could have stopped the evil Eden City people reaching out and taking what they wanted.

So why do I want to stay in this cruel and crumbling city?

I remembered that Theus will be coming to the city for his first visit in 1858. I've decided I'd like to see him one more time. Though he won't know me... he won't have met me. And anyway, I'm an old woman now, not the young girl who helped him free a princess.

But I did go to the Temple of the Hero one day. I wanted to see just who this hero was.

The temple was decayed and dusty. A faded sign said, "Caretaker wanted. Apply to Mayor Mucklethrift".

I walked in.

The statue stood under its tattered cloth. I pulled the cloth off the carved, stone figure and looked at the face.

I was shocked. And puzzled. And pleased. And sad.

I covered it up again and went to the City Hall.

I got myself the job of caretaker. I care a lot.

Theus will return within the year.

I hope I live long enough to see him. I know he won't find the end of his quest there because in his time he's already been to 1858 and failed.

The answer lies somewhere in the past. People like me can't go back.

But I pray, by whatever gods there may be, that Theus finds what he's looking for.

I know he will. I'm sure he will.

GLOSSARY

Achilles: A strong and fearless warrior in the Greek war against the Trojans. As an infant his mother dipped him into the River Styx, which made him invulnerable everywhere but the heel by which she held him.

The Avenger/ The Fury: An eagle with god-given powers, it was commanded by Zeus to rip out Prometheus's liver every day.

Hecatonchires: A giant Greek monster of incredible strength and ferocity. It had one hundred hands and fifty heads.

Helen: The queen of Sparta. She was so beautiful men would start wars to be with her. When she was kidnapped by Paris it started the Trojan war.

Hera: The queen of the Olympian deities. She was a daughter of Cronus and Rhea, and wife and sister of Zeus. Hera was mainly worshipped as a goddess of marriage and birth.

Hermes: The son of Zeus and the messenger of the gods. It was his duty to guide the souls of the dead down to the Underworld.

Paris: The king of Troy. He kidnapped Helen the queen of Sparta which started the Trojan war.

Polyxena: A beautiful Trojan princess, the youngest daughter of King Priam.

Prometheus: A Titan who stole fire from Zeus and the gods. In punishment, Zeus commanded that Prometheus be chained for eternity in the Caucasus. There, an eagle would eat his liver, and each day the liver would be renewed, making the punishment endless.

Troy: A legendary city during the period of Ancient Greece. It was the scene of the Trojan war which lasted several years.

Zeus: The youngest son of Cronus and Rhea, he was the supreme ruler of Mount Olympus and of the Pantheon of gods who resided there. He upheld law, justice and morals, and was the spiritual leader of both gods and men.

**A selected list of titles available from
Kingfisher, an imprint of Macmillan Children's Books**

The prices shown below are correct at the time of going to press. However, Macmillan Publishers reserves the right to show new retail prices on covers, which may differ from those previously advertised.

Terry Deary
The Fire Thief	ISBN:978-0-7534-1702-7	£5.99
The Fire Thief Fights Back	ISBN:978-0-7534-1701-0	£5.99

Malcolm Rose
Traces: Blood Brother	ISBN:978-0-7534-1541-2	£5.99
Traces: Double Check	ISBN:978-0-7534-1492-7	£5.99
Traces: Final Lap	ISBN:978-0-7534-1340-1	£5.99
Traces: Framed!	ISBN:978-0-7534-1493-4	£5.99
Traces: Lost Bullet	ISBN:978-0-7534-1494-1	£5.99
Traces: Roll Call	ISBN:978-0-7534-1495-8	£5.99

All Pan Macmillan titles can be ordered from our website, www.panmacmillan.com, or from your local bookshop and are also available by post from:

Bookpost, PO Box 29, Douglas, Isle of Man IM99 1BQ
Credit cards accepted. For details:
Telephone: 01624 677237
Fax: 01624 670 923
Email: bookshop@enterprise.net
www.bookpost.co.uk
Free postage and packing in the United Kingdom